Praise for
# *Once Upon A Christmas*

Oscar Wilde wrote, "Memory is the diary that we all carry about with us." If this is so, Richard Smith's anthology of his Christmas-themed prose represents a personal diary that he graciously shares with us.

Alternating and blending reality and fantasy, Smith's tales of Christmas weave a sentimental tapestry of times gone by, of people, places, and events that forged his life experiences and nurtured his imaginary realm. Through his stories we can relate vicariously and meld our own experiences with the author's wit, wisdom, and powers of observation.

This work is a delightful mosaic of holiday musings that will attract the reader like a moth to a porch light. Christmas is not just a time, but a frame of mind built from the bricks of personal memories and imaginary fantasies. This book provides the mortar.

**—John Gendron,** Mesa, Arizona

We love Christmas, and one of the things we love most is our Christmas story from Dick Smith. About the first of December, we start watching out our window to see Dick riding on his bicycle to deliver our story. We never know what to expect. Some years, the story will be humorous, sometimes sentimental, and then there are those that contain a bit of both. All are equally enjoyed, and we are looking forward to reading them all again in *Once Upon A Christmas*.

**—Loren and Judy Hanson,** Bradenton, Florida

On our book shelf is a red notebook. The title, "Christmas Stories. Dick Smith." Inside are twenty-two stories dating from the first we received in 1994, each a Christmas gift from the author. We all have our stories. Dick has shared many of his so that we can find ourselves in them. Fun, clever, surprising, thoughtful, touching stories. Oh, yes, with a bit of the Blarney.

**—Elaine Lohr,** Madison, Wisconsin

Dick's Christmas stories, often set in small-town America, much like his own home town, are charming, funny, and thought-provoking, filled with people like those I've known. His gift for telling a good story has been the gift he has given to friends, family, and neighbors every Christmas for twenty-five years. I have looked forward to reading his stories, wondering what he will come up with this year. Now lucky readers everywhere can enjoy this holiday treat.

—**Vivian Powless**, Edina, Minnesota


Engrossing, enticing, sometimes poignant, and frequently hilarious, this accomplished author and skilled storyteller's collection of Christmas narratives is sure to entertain and captivate. In fact, perhaps as a bonus, it may restore a delicious faded memory from the reader's past, as it did for me. Of special interest, the introductions to his stories provide a glimpse of how the characters, plot, and setting of each were chosen. By way of a medley of reminiscences, imaginative fiction, and shrewd observations, it is a marvelous trip. This author's Christmas gift is very certain to leave you wishing for more and one that can be enjoyed again and again any time of the year.

—**Marie Bone**, Bradenton, Florida


One of the first people we met shortly after we moved into our Florida condominium community was the author Richard Smith. Little did we know at the time that he would provide one of the most anticipated events at the start of each holiday season, his annual Christmas story.

Over time, his stories became legendary in our community as he spun his eclectic tales, many grounded in his personal experiences, others purely fictional but just as captivating. We could hardly wait to open the brown 8.5 x 11 inch envelope we found in our screen door early each December to see what he had conjured up for that year.

As you will see as you read this book, his stories never fail to stir the emotions or tickle the funny bone, and in some cases both.

—**Jack and Darlene Wymer**, Bradenton, Florida
Perico Bay Club residents for twenty-eight years

Christmas Eve has always been the calm before the storm that is Christmas day. One of my favorite family traditions is Christmas Eve story time. We gather as a family around a cozy fire to read aloud the annual story written by my grandfather, Dr. Richard J. Smith.

The stories are rich with Wisconsin history, embracing life's twists and turns and a poem sprinkled in here and there. Reading the story is a wonderful way to feel close as a family, even if we can't geographically be together during the holidays. By the end of the story, we have all laughed and shed a few tears.

—**Katie Larson**, Plymouth, Minnesota

*Once Upon a Christmas:*
*A Collection of Short Stories*
by Richard J. Smith, Ph.D.

© Copyright 2016 Richard J. Smith, Ph.D.

ISBN 978-1-63393-378-1

All rights reserved. No part of this publication may be reproduced, stored in a retrieval system, or transmitted in any form or by any means – electronic, mechanical, photocopy, recording, or any other – except for brief quotations in printed reviews, without the prior written permission of the author.

Published by

210 60th Street
Virginia Beach, VA 23451
800-435-4811
www.koehlerbooks.com

*To my friend, Sister Regis. May all your Christmases be merry.*

*Dick Sth*

# Once Upon a Christmas

*A Collection of Short Stories*

*Richard J. Smith, Ph.D.*

VIRGINIA BEACH
CAPE CHARLES

# *Dedication*

*To all who love and live the spirt of Christmas*

# Table of Contents

❄ ❄ ❄

INTRODUCTION . . . . . . . . . . . . . . . . . . . 5

PA BUYS A TAVERN . . . . . . . . . . . . . . . . 9

SENT TO SCHOOL . . . . . . . . . . . . . . . . . 18

CHRISTMAS IS COMING AND SO ARE WE. . . 27

A CHRISTMAS SECRET . . . . . . . . . . . . . . 37

A LITTLE CHRISTMAS MAGIC . . . . . . . . . . 43

GRANDFATHER LIU'S CHRISTMAS GIFT . . . . 55

CHRISTMAS LIGHT . . . . . . . . . . . . . . . . 66

THE DAY BEFORE CHRISTMAS VACATION . . 72

BIRDS FLY OVER THE RAINBOW . . . . . . . . 83

I BEGIN MY CAREER . . . . . . . . . . . . . . . 96

THE CHRISTMAS TRUCE OF 2017 . . . . . . . 103

ACKNOWLEDGMENTS . . . . . . . . . . . . . . 108

ABOUT THE AUTHOR. . . . . . . . . . . . . . 109

# *Introduction*

INTRODUCTIONS TO BOOKS are written to prepare readers for what they are getting into. They also introduce authors to their readers. So, as we used to say in my home town in northern Wisconsin, "I'm pleased to make your acquaintance."

At this sitting, I am eighty-six years old and have been writing seriously since the third grade when I won the contest for the best Christmas poem in my class. I still remember that poem and Sister Germaine asking me to come to the front of the room and read it to those who lost the contest.

> *Three wise men saw it from afar,*
> *A large and shiny Christmas star.*
> *They rode their camels fast as they were able*
> *And came upon a humble stable.*
> *Inside was a family with a baby boy,*
> *But the wise men didn't bring a toy.*
> *They brought gifts fit for a king,*
> *And they could hear the angels sing.*
> *Because the baby was Jesus, the king of them all.*
> *And he still is with us, winter, spring, summer and fall.*
> *And every Christmas we kneel and pray.*
> *And that's why we have Christmas day.*

The rest of the class read their poems too, but, in my humble opinion, none came close to mine.

Since then I have written college textbooks, instructional materials for classroom use, and articles for professional journals. About a year ago, I came out of retirement and wrote *Life After Eighty,* a personal perspective of preparing for old age.

Now I have written this book of Christmas stories and the accompanying comments. When you finish reading them, you will know me much better, and hopefully, you will have been cheerfully entertained or inspired.

When I write a story, I do so without an outline. I begin with a character, an event, or a setting and let the "map" unfold as I travel. The journey is always enjoyable, and somehow, I arrive at a destination. After many years of writing college textbooks and articles for professional journals, I find letting my pen go where it will makes me feel much like a professional golfer must feel playing nine holes just for the fun of it.

Writing poetry is also a spontaneous adventure for me. The words and the "music" fill my head and find exit through the movement of my hand holding a pen. Sometimes what appears on the paper is pretty good. And sometimes, well, I always write with a wastebasket by my side.

Writing extemporaneously as I do has a shortcoming: titles elude me. I cannot begin with a title as I am not sure just where I am going, and affixing a title to where I have been always seems to shortchange the scenery along the way. Editors I have been guided by through the years were always short on praise for the titles I concocted.

Among some of the characters upon which my concoctions are founded are students who hold a place dear to me. I spent nearly sixty years of my life in schools, either as a student or as a teacher. I know firsthand that some teachers are life preservers for kids who are drowning or caught up in a current carrying them into rough water. I also know that schools don't work for all kids and that some people are more in control of their lives than others.

When I retired in 1990 after thirty-eight years as a classroom teacher, a public school administrator, and a professor of education, our country was still adjusting to the integration of schools and was just beginning to develop curricula for diversity in education. Twenty-six years later, we are still at it.

One story in this collection explores that topic head-on, drawing upon my experiences as a teacher of remedial reading. I learned while teaching these kids that they all come to school from different home environments and with different motivations and capabilities for learning to read. In another of my reveries, *I Begin My Career,* I draw from my first year of my first teaching position. I hope you will enjoy the read as much as I enjoy the memory.

*Birds Fly Over the Rainbow*, another musing based on distant memory, is also based upon good that I have seen in classrooms. The story is fiction, but it is real to me. *Birds Fly Over* is, at its root, a story of hope. In almost every school there is a teacher who gets beneath the wings of her students and helps them fly over rainbows.

I invite you to ride along with me in pursuit of these Christmas stories. Should you tire of the chase, you have my permission to leave these pages. But I hope you will not, for readers never know when an ending may redeem a beginning or a middle.

For starters, let's see if together we can perform a little Christmas magic. Like the magician who relies on your willingness to accept illusion as reality and the hypnotist who takes you to a different level of consciousness, I will attempt to transport you to a different realm. And also like the magician and the hypnotist, I will require your complete attention and cooperation. If you agree to these terms, we are ready to depart.

The present is receding from your consciousness. Reality is being suspended. From reality to fantasy, from fact to fiction, from here to there. Logic and reason are being trumped by trickery and fakery. Don't resist. Don't hold back. Follow my words. You are embarking on a Christmas tide.

Listen to my voice. Believe what you hear. Do not struggle as you sense your transformation occurring. You are now drifting to years long past. Breathe deeply. Release your tension. Let yourself drift. Feel the breezes of time loosening your moorings. Let yourself sail with me to earlier times—see yourself as a young adult—now a teenager with energy, stamina, no grey hair.

Farther back. A little farther still. Whoa! Far enough.

Close your eyes and rest for a minute. Your journey is complete. When you open your eyes, you will see yourself as . . . *A Child Again!*

But alas, even children must not be boldly lied to, so I start with an admission: I admit to embellishing some of the events and even adding a few that didn't really happen. With some exceptions, the actual details of our lives are not as interesting to others as we imagine them to be. So I "pinched" the truth here and there to add a little color

I hope my musings stir some of your own memories or provoke some thoughts or elicit some smiles and frowns and perhaps conjure a laugh or a tear. I hope you will come to know more about yourself through my journeys, imagined and real.

So let's get on with it, but before you do, let me wish you a very *Merry Christmas.* Here's a poem I wrote to put you in the mood. I call it *The Words of Christmas:*

*Speak softly, for it is Christmas and your words*
*Should fall as snowflakes to the ground.*
*Speak words that comfort, for it is Christmas, and*
*Your words should dress the wounds of those in pain.*

*Listen patiently to the sorrows of others, for*
*It is Christmas and those who sorrow need your ear.*
*Offer forgiveness to your offenders at Christmas,*
*For Christmas is a time to give the gift of peace.*

*Open your ears and mind to the beliefs of others at*
*Christmas, for an open mind is the doorway to understanding.*
*Avoid bold assertions at Christmas, for strident*
*Speech is displeasing to the ear and disquieting to the soul.*

*Invite the reticent to speak, for it is Christmas*
*And they too have words worth hearing.*
*Find and give the joy and love of Christmas with tongue*
*    and ear*
*For words are who we are and how we pray.*

# *Pa Buys a Tavern*

PA DIED AT the age of ninety-seven, seven years later than he thought he would.

He and Ma were the same age, had been together since they were teenagers, and always figured they would go out together. Ma died at ninety, and he wanted to go along. "I don't know why I'm hangin' around so long," he told me once when we were drinking a beer together.

I'll say this about Ma and Pa, they had a high regard for the proper celebration of Christmas. And even when times were tough, they saw to it that I got my new flannel shirts, corduroy pants, and plaid mackinaw. Christmases were always cold in Wisconsin. I got toys and other stuff, too, but they were different every year. I don't remember all of the gifts I received, but I do remember when Pa bought a tavern.

Pa was passed over for a foreman opening at the mill because he didn't have a high school education, so he decided to go into business for himself. Against Ma's wishes he bought a tavern.

"You'll drink up all the profits," Ma predicted (with some reason, because Pa could toss 'em down with the best of them).

The tavern Pa bought was a dump that hadn't turned a profit since the days when area farmers came to town Saturday nights to shop and lumberjacks came in from the woods to get drunk and fight. When preachers complained that Saturday night shopping kept their flock away from Sunday church, the merchants stayed open Friday nights instead.

❄ ❄ ❄

That's what started the Friday night tavern fish fry; food merchants wanted to appease the hunger of Roman Catholic shoppers who were not permitted to eat meat on Fridays. After he opened the tavern, Pa said he was glad the church never came down on drinking Menominee Silver Cream Beer with a fish fry.

I don't think Pa had any money for a down payment on the place. My hunch is the bank would have financed Jack the Ripper if he'd promise to give up his murdering ways, fix the place up, and make a mortgage payment now and then, which was more than the previous owner did.

When Ma asked what we were going to do with such a big place, Pa explained he had big plans. He wanted to put in some booths and that we'd be living in the quarters upstairs. Old-timers claimed the upstairs rooms once housed a "stable of fillies for the lumberjacks to ride when they came to town to shop on Saturday nights." I couldn't imagine how horses got up and down those rickety back steps until I figured out that the lumberjacks must have carried them.

"But the upstairs is too big for us," Ma protested.

"Not with Grandpa here," Pa explained again. "With Grandma gone and us with all this room, there's no use for Grandpa to live alone in the old farm house. We can rent that out or sell it."

I could see Ma wasn't about to dance her Irish jig to celebrate the news, but she didn't argue because she knew my grandpa was probably already upstairs unpacking.

Pa called the place Smitty's Bar, and he turned out to be a good business man. There was an unwritten rule for bartenders in those days that "the house" always bought the third drink; buy two, get one on the house. However, if you accepted the third drink, you had to buy another and include one for the bartender. The bartender never bought the last drink unless it was closing time.

Every tavern goer and every bartender knew the rules.

Pa bent the rules a little. Sometimes he bought the second drink, sometimes the first, sometimes the fourth and fifth. He kept our stools filled with customers not wanting to leave in case Pa bought the next round, like slot machine players always thinking the next spin will trigger a payout. Moreover, Pa had Ma come in from the kitchen at different times with free cheese and sausage and rye bread. And sometimes she brought in pickled pigs feet or pickled hard-boiled eggs. Customers hung around because they never knew when Ma would make her entrance, and nobody wanted to miss the free lunch.

Since Grandpa didn't have much work to do, he and I spent a lot of time together. It was he who set me free of the notion that lumberjacks carried horses up and down the back steps. Grandpa could have taught Masters and Johnson a thing or two about sex. He also taught me how to make a slingshot from a forked tree branch and bicycle inner-tube strips.

"We'll get us some rats," he told me. Rats were a constant in the cellars and alleys all over town and especially around anyplace that sold food.

Our tavern was only a couple of hundred yards from the Menominee River. Freighters plying the Great Lakes regularly sailed from Lake Michigan into Green Bay and then up the Menominee River, where they unloaded huge piles of coal and took away huge loads of sugar beets.

Folklore had it that rats came off those freighters, swam across the river, and joined earlier immigrant relatives in our cellars and alleys. Anyone who could pick off a swimming rat with a slingshot became somewhat of a hero, and many claimed they had stopped the invading hordes by the dozens and even the hundreds.

Grandpa and I sat on our side of the river with our slingshots loaded many a summer afternoon and never saw a rat. But I heard Grandpa tell some men at the bar one morning that he and I were going down to the river again that afternoon to get us some more rats.

About a year after Pa opened Smitty's Bar, he began hearing about the wonderful Friday night fish fries Norman's Bar was putting out for thirty cents, five cents more than Pa was charging. So Pa gave one of his regulars thirty cents and sent him down to Norman's about nine o'clock to find out what was so special about his fish fry.

The report came back near midnight. The scout had to wait almost two hours for a booth to free up. He drank six beers while waiting at the bar, so Pa owed him another thirty cents. Norman's perch, baked beans, and rye bread were the same, but he also served a generous helping of French fried potatoes.

Pa retaliated. Every Friday afternoon I got the job of peeling enough spuds for Ma to cook for our fish fries that Pa now charged thirty-five cents for. The price which included a free beer. Norman lost customers, Pa made the profit on the beer as well as the fish fry, and nobody figured out they were paying for the free beer when they coughed up thirty-five cents for the food.

One Friday afternoon after school, I was peeling potatoes in the kitchen and thinking about Christmas vacation coming up. Grandpa was helping me. Suddenly he shot up in the air like the Human Cannonball at the County Fair. "My God!" he yelled. "Look at the size of that rat!" He was pointing down at where his feet had been. I watched him until he landed, and then I looked at where he'd been pointing. Grandpa's explosive elevation had been triggered by a small cat—not a large rat—rubbing against his leg. I figure Grandpa was always worried that some rat would try to get revenge for all its relatives Grandpa had lied about killing with a slingshot.

Now I had never desired a cat as a pet. But I had prayed nightly, and sometimes in school when things got dull, that Pa would relent and let me have a dog. I pleaded with Pa, who explained his refusal. "You gotta male, he's always bitin' the milkman or the mailman or the iceman, someone you gotta have comin' around all the time. You gotta bitch, she's always comin' home with a belly full of pups. There ain't no winnin' with a damn dog." (Grandpa had to set me straight on the part about the bitch.)

But I dreamed of owning a dog all the time. If I had a white dog, I would name it Silver after the Lone Ranger's horse. If I had a brown dog, I would name it Scout after Tonto's horse. And if I had a black dog, I would name it Blackie. Color was not an important factor. I just really wanted a dog—any dog—but when divine providence dropped that stray cat in the kitchen into my lap, I figured I'd make do until Pa changed his mind about a dog. "I'm gonna keep him," I said to Grandpa. "A stray cat's better than nothin'."

"That there cat ain't no stray," Grandpa pronounced. "Thatn's been well-fed and kept indoors." The cat had its eyes mostly shut and was licking at its paws as if Grandpa and I weren't even there. "He don't look like much of a mouser, but I'll square it with your pa if you wanna keep him—and don't tell nobody he wandered in here."

"What'll I call him?" I asked Grandpa. Neither Silver nor Scout seemed to fit; and since he was grey and white, Blackie was out of the question.

"That there cat belonged to somebody and like as not has got a name already," Grandpa said. I failed to see how that was going to help me choose a name until Grandpa continued. "You can't call him nothin' else. A cat with more'n one name'll never chase mice, and we sure as hell need us a mouser. Too bad he ain't a she. No Tommy can catch mice like a female."

"Then what'll I call him?" I tried again.

Grandpa thought a moment; then he said, "Call him Cat. That ain't a name."

So Cat it was. And if nobody saw him and claimed him, I had me a pet.

When I looked down, I saw that Cat had fallen asleep next to my potato bucket, so I peeled real quietly so as not to awaken Cat. When I finished the bucketful, I looked up and saw Grandpa was still there, watching me.

"You know, Dickie," he said, "the bad thing about being old is you ain't a somebody no more." Then he smiled, and his eyes kind of smiled, too. "You're keepin' me a somebody, boy." Many years passed before I knew what he had meant.

Pa said I could keep Cat on two conditions: "He earns his keep by catchin' mice, and nobody comes around sayin' they lost a cat that looks like him." So he was all mine!

"Thanks, Pa. Thanks a lot."

Before Cat joined our family, we had mousetraps scattered all over our upstairs apartment and the tavern kitchen. Nothing much happened during the day, but all night long those traps caught mice. I remember lying in bed in the dark, hearing the traps snap shut one after another, each one hanging on to the neck of a furry mouse with its nose on the cheese bait:

> *The best laid schemes o' mice an' men*
> *Gang aft agley,*
> *An' lea'e us naught but grief an' pain*
> *For promised joy!*

Sometimes, Grandpa or Ma or Pa got up to release the victims and reset the traps. So they were especially happy when Cat turned out to be an excellent mouser.

"Only cat I ever knew was a better mouser than this'n was a old female tiger cat we had on the farm. By God, she'd chase a mouse into a pile a horse manure, drag it out, lick it clean, and swallow it down head first, tail wigglin' like hell all the way down. And Dickie's cat is damned near as good!"

So one of the conditions for my keeping Cat was met. But not Pa's requirement that the original owner not show up. About a month after I adopted Cat, Gus Gustafson was drinking a beer at the bar and spied Cat licking his paws in one of the booths Pa put in for Friday night fish fries.

"Hoo, boy!" Gus whooped. "Where you get dat cat?"

"Just wandered in," Pa answered. "Why? You see him before?"

"You damn betcha. That there's my cat. The Mrs. left the door open shakin' out rugs 'bout a month ago, and I ain't seen dat devil since."

"You real sure about that, Gus?" Pa asked.

"You damn betcha I'm sure. That there's the meanest cat ever lived. Scratchin' and bitin' at me 'til I'm about to shoot the bastard. Never caught a mouse neither."

Pa didn't say anything until he'd thought awhile. Then he said, "You know, Gus, that cat's still a mean son of a bitch, and he wouldn't know it if a mouse crawled up his ass, but him and the kid get along real good." Then Pa rubbed his chin and pulled on his ear lobe like he was having a hard time making up his mind. "Tell you what, Gus. You say the word, and I'll take that good-for-nothin' cat off your hands." Gus didn't say anything, so Pa added, "And give you and the misses a fish fry and couple beers on the house Friday night."

"Throw in a Schnapps, too?" Gus bargained. Pa agreed.

"By the way," Pa asked, "what's his name?"

"Never gived him a name," Gus replied. "Just called him the first cuss word come to mind."

Grandpa was at the end of the bar and heard it all. He told me about it, word for word, and he said Pa and Gus even shook hands on the deal. So I had me a cat now with no contingencies. And best of all, now I could give Cat a real name. But somehow Cat was better than any other name I could think of, so I just left it at that. Pa has never told about the deal he made with Gus.

❄ ❄ ❄

The week before Christmas was the best week of the year for Main Street taverns. The stores stayed open until nine o'clock every night except Sunday, and while the women folks shopped at Gambles and J.C. Penney and Kinney Shoes and Stancil's Department Store, their husbands got tired of shopping and waited for them at Norman's or Smitty's. The wives stopped by at nine o'clock to fetch their husbands and, since it was the holidays, also had a drink. It was usually a whiskey and sweet soda or whiskey and sour soda that cost twenty cents, eight cents profit. By this time their husbands were full of beer and ordered a Peppermint Schnapps "for the road." That was also twenty cents. The cash register rang like Santa's sleigh bells the week before Christmas.

Christmas Eve the stores all closed at five o'clock, and at six (or seven), so did the taverns.

The Christmas Eve I'll never forget Ma and Pa and Grandpa were tired out and a little tipsy from drinking so much Christmas cheer with their regulars. They just wanted to lock up downstairs and go to bed right after supper. That suited me fine because I was only seven years old and wanted to be sure Santa didn't pass us by due to the fact our lights were on.

I snuggled between my flannel sheets with Cat lying on my feet. I gave him a couple of bounces from under the covers just to let him know I knew he was there. I must have fallen asleep right away because I had been dreaming when I heard Cat growling and no longer felt his weight. I sat up and looked into the darkness, trying to locate him. "Get back here, Cat!" I called, but not too loud so as not to awaken Ma and Pa and Grandpa.

Suddenly Cat's growls became frantic cries and shrieks, and I could tell he was bouncing around the room like a golf ball dropped on cement. I got the light on in time to see him leap at the closed door with his claws out so far he stuck there. Then Pa yelled, "What the hell's goin' on in there?"

I yelled back, "Cat's goin' nuts in here, Pa. I'm scared!

Pretty soon I heard Ma yell, "I smell smoke!"

And then Grandpa hollered, "Everybody get the hell outta here!"

Pa flung open my door, and Cat and I beat it out of there. Ma was already downstairs with her flashlight beam piercing the smoke, talking on the telephone to the night watchman at the mill. "Blow the whistle, Hank! We got us a fire over here at Smitty's."

It took the volunteer firefighters thirty-five minutes to get to the station, start up the truck, drive it the six blocks down Main Street, siren going full blast, and come busting in our front door. They had been drinking a little Christmas cheer, too. By that time Pa had found a smoldering cigarette between the stuffed horsehide seat and the back of one of our new booths and doused it with a pail of water.

"Sorry about the fuss, boys," he said to the volunteers in their big coats, pointed hats, and rubber boots. "How about a couple beers for your trouble?" They weren't about to turn down a free beer on Christmas Eve, so they headed for the bar. Ma said I should stay downstairs with the men while she opened the windows upstairs to clear out the smoke smell.

The party lasted about an hour, and when I got upstairs, Santa Claus had come, and all my presents were under the tree. Ma swore she didn't see him, but for the life of me I couldn't figure out how Santa got by Ma and did his work without her seeing him. Even Grandpa pleaded ignorance on that one.

❄ ❄ ❄

Well, that's about the end of the Christmas memory, except for one more thing. On a Friday afternoon that spring, I was peeling potatoes on the back porch when Cat decided to take a stroll down the street. She came home a week later with a "belly full of kittens."

I was glad I hadn't changed her name when I had the chance, because I probably would have named her Tommy or some other boy name.

# *Sent To School*

THIS NEXT STORY picks up just about where the last one left off.

When Cat came home "with a bellyful of kittens," Pa said Cat could stay, but the kittens had to go, even though they came out of a good mouser.

"One cat in the place is enough," Pa declared; and although Ma took my part about keeping one with the markings of Cat, Pa stood his ground. "We got us a business here," he said, "servin' food Friday nights. All it takes is one hair in a fish fry to send our customers to Norman's Bar. Be dammed if I'll lose business over a cat, especially to a Lutheran."

Now, to understand Pa's argument, you have to know that Pa could not tolerate a hair of any kind in his food. You also have to know that our small town was pretty much divided between Catholics and Lutherans in just about everything. They bickered in matters of which religion was the only true path to salvation to matters as small as who gave bigger portions at their ice cream socials, even though neither had ever been to the other's to know for sure.

Given a choice, Lutherans did business with Lutherans and Catholics with Catholics. Since most of the politicians, businessmen, and farmers who patronized Smitty's Bar were Irish Catholic, Pa traded on the fact that Norman's Bar at the other end of Main Street was owned and operated by a Lutheran.

But Pa never revealed that he was not a Catholic. He wasn't a Lutheran either; so, as Ma liked to point out to him, he was a "nothing" when it came to religious preference. Most people thought Pa was a Catholic because he was married to Ma, and "mixed marriages in northeastern Wisconsin in the 1930's were rare birds." Customers who went to early mass and didn't see Pa there assumed he went to late mass and vice versa. Ma blamed Pa for being a hypocrite when he hid behind her religion for business reasons and, on more than one occasion, told him, "If you're going to talk like a Catholic, join the Church."

You should probably have another little piece of history here. Pa was baptized a Lutheran, but the water must have run off his head too fast, because he never put much stock in Lutheranism or any other "ism." He used to say, "You can't trust a man with religion any more than you can trust one without it." He loved Ma, but not enough to join her church; and Ma loved the Catholic church, but not enough to give up Pa for it. So Pa took some instructions from the parish priest and promised "to raise any children issuing from the marriage in the Catholic faith." And when I issued from the marriage, there I was, half-Catholic, half-nothing and already promised to Our Lady of Lourdes Elementary School.

So when it was time for me to get more education than I was getting from Grandpa and from eavesdropping on the men sitting at the bar, I was, at a very early age, handed over to the School Sisters of Notre Dame. Nothing at Smitty's Bar had prepared me for my first encounter with women who had taken vows of poverty, chastity, and obedience so they could boss around little kids. After the first day, I told Pa I had made up my mind I wasn't going back to that school. But the promise he made to Ma's priest was still stuck in his head, and he un-made my mind before I could say, "Hail Mary."

One vow my teachers had not taken was tolerance. There was no slipping between the cracks with the School Sisters of Notre Dame. They added an eleventh commandment to God's ten: "Obey the School Sisters of Notre Dame, for God and your parents have put them in charge." But they and I were a good match. They had a lot to teach, and I had a lot to learn.

One thing I learned was how to memorize. The Baltimore Catechism was central to my early religious instruction, and we were required to recite from memory answers to questions beginning with, "Who made me?" That was the easiest one, but I'm not sure Pa would have agreed with the answer. Anyway, the practice in memorizing the Baltimore Catechism in English proved to be good training for memorizing the Prayers at the Foot of the Altar in Latin when I was in the fourth grade. And that's where this story goes next.

Charles Dickens begins *A Tale of Two Cities* with the lines, "It was the best of times and the worst of times." Well, that's the way it was with me in the fourth grade, but the other way around. First of all, Grandpa had a stroke. When he got home from the hospital, he had some paralysis, and he started calling me by Pa's name and forgetting to go to the toilet when he needed to. Ma said he was getting "funny in the head" and too much for her to handle. So he went off to the nursing home in Peshtigo, the one near his old farm.

And then Cat died. Actually, she was killed by a family of raccoons that were hanging out in an old shack down by the river. She got out one night through a broken basement window and came home the next morning all bit up and smelling like raccoon. Pa felt her all over with soft hands and said, "She's pretty banged up, son. You go off to school now, and I'll take care of things here." I never saw Cat again, never asked Pa just how he took care of "things," and he never told me. Some things are better left unsaid, I guess.

So there I was, a half-Catholic, half-nothing boy in an all Catholic school without Grandpa and Cat and no brothers or sisters. But that lonely-orphan feeling was soon to change. And what happened next made my year in fourth grade "the best of times."

Sister Mary Rose selected, trained and supervised the altar boys at Our Lady of Lourdes. She had been informed by my classroom teacher, Sister Lewis, that I was a good oral reader and dependable. "Richard," Sister Rose asked, "would you like to join the Society of Acolytes in the Service of the Lord?" Now, who could turn down an invitation like that? Ma lit up with pride when I told her, and Pa just snorted, "Getting' awful deep into that religion stuff."

I suppose learning to be an altar boy from Sister Mary

Rose was a lot like boot camp in the military. In addition to memorizing the mass prayers in Latin, I had to learn how to light the altar candles, how to pour water and wine from cruets into the priest's chalice, which priest preferred more wine than water, how to ring the bells at Consecration, how to hold a paten under the chin of a communicant without lacerating the larynx, how to fire up an incense briquette without burning the church down, and that the altar wine in the cupboard of the sacristy was for the priest only and was never without the eye of God upon it.

Near the middle of November I was pronounced "ready to serve" by Sister Rose and was assigned a weekday low mass with an experienced partner, Timmy McNary, whose father was a good customer of Pa's. My surplice wasn't on straight, I rang the Consecration bells too long, nearly tripped on my cassock moving the priest's missal from the right to the left side of the altar, and banged Gus Gustafson in the throat with the paten at the communion rail. Other than that, Sister said I did fine; and after Father left the sacristy, Timmy opened the wine cupboard, took a tiny sip out of one of the bottles, and poured in several drops of water to replace it. I declined his offer to "take one for yourself" on the grounds that I wouldn't want to confess it on Saturday. Timmy said it was only a venial sin and therefore not worthy of taking Father's time in the confessional, what with all the mortal sins he'd be dealing with. Timmy grew up to be a lawyer.

Christmas was drawing near, and Sister Rose was having trouble recruiting mass servers for vacation weekdays. She was having even bigger trouble finding someone for the six a.m. Christmas mass in the convent chapel. Serving six a.m. mass in that small chapel, with that small altar, with Sister Rose, your other teachers, the high school sisters, and even Sister Fortunata, the principal of the whole school watching your every move, was not an appealing beginning to an elementary school boy's Christmas morning. In addition, servers in the convent chapel worked alone with the priest—one priest, one altar boy, and about twenty School Sisters of Notre Dame in full dress uniform. Merry Christmas!

One by one, "Acolytes in the Service of the Lord" proffered their excuses:

- "I gotta go to church with my family on Christmas, Sister."
- "At six in the morning we're openin' presents at my grandma's sister."
- "My Ma's singin' in the choir at midnight mass, and I gotta hear her sing, Sister."
- "I think we're gonna be gone for Christmas. Maybe to Menominee. Or Peshtigo, or somewhere else."

I listened to Sister Mary Rose counter-argue, urge her boys to remember the grace that comes with doing the Lord's work regardless of inconvenience, and finally plead for some boy to assist Father at six a.m. Christmas Mass in the convent chapel. Suddenly, I, without good reason, wanted to be that boy. Perhaps it was the same spirit that prompted me many years later to agree to be president of my condominium association. I raised my hand and volunteered, "I'll do it, Sister."

Later, when I told Ma and Pa at the supper table about my volunteering, I couldn't help but wonder why I had done such a foolish thing. Pa wondered, too, and he pointed out it was still "dammed dark" at five in the morning when I'd have to get up, and it would likely be "snowin' and cold as an Eskimo's ass." I can tell you I was plenty worried, but saw no way of backing out of my responsibility. That would probably be a sin no priest could ever forgive.

My mind left that problem when Ma asked what I'd like Santa to bring me that year. I didn't really still believe in Santa Claus, but then again I didn't completely not believe either. The religious teaching I was receiving was a lot about miracles and the importance of accepting the miraculous on faith, so sometimes I just stretched my faith a little to get Santa under that net, too.

Right off, I stated my strong and hopeful desire for a dog, a dog to play with now that Grandpa and Cat were gone and I had no brothers or sister, a dog I would take complete care of so my parents wouldn't have to do one little thing for it, a dog with short hair that wouldn't fall out and get into customers' fish fries.

Pa asked how I'd feel if "Old Whiskers" brought me a BB gun instead. I thought a moment before I answered, because a BB gun would be a whole lot better for shooting river rats than a sling shot. And I didn't want how I answered Pa's question to cut me out of both. So I said slowly, "Well, a BB gun would be . . . second." Then I said fast, "But a dog would be first. One with short hair."

Pa smiled and said, "I guess we'll just have to wait and see what the old guy brings. Right, Ma?" When Ma smiled back, I took it for a sign I was going to get one or the other.

Ma said she would set an alarm clock and wake me up at five Christmas morning. "I'd drive you," she said, "only I never did get around to learning how. And I wouldn't count on your Pa. He don't much like the idea of you being an altar boy in the first place. But I'm so proud of you, honey. I know you'll do just fine."

Christmas Eve I went to bed a bundle of nerves. It had turned cold, below zero, and the wind was howling like a wolf outside. I didn't much like the prospect of hiking the twelve blocks to the convent even though I knew Ma would have me buttoned, wrapped in scarves, and ear-muffed like the mummy in our geography book. And I just knew Pa had no intention of getting me a dog, even one with short hair. But most of all, I was scared about being the only altar boy at Christmas morning mass in the convent chapel, with the first row of nuns so close they could hear the way I mumbled most of the Suscipiat prayer without really saying the words. I fell asleep rehearsing the prayers at the foot of the altar in Latin.

Christmas morning Ma woke me up, but Pa was waiting for me in the kitchen. He surprised me by saying, "I'm drivin' you down to those sisters' place. No man should be walkin' that far this time of day in this weather, let alone a kid. The priest likely won't show up."

I followed Pa out the back door to the '35 Ford that never got parked in a garage because we didn't have one. The car was so cold, Pa had a hard time moving the stick shift on the floor into neutral. Holding the clutch down with his left foot, he pumped the accelerator with his right foot about twenty times, his head and upper body bobbing with each pump. Finally he pulled out the choke on the dashboard, moved his foot from the accelerator pedal to the starter button and stepped on it. At first, nothing but the sound of the starter grinding. Then the engine made a low, guttural, humming sound. It choked, coughed, sputtered, hummed again, and finally caught. The whole car shook, the engine trying to catch a rhythm, like a fibrillating heart. Pa pushed in the choke, let out the clutch, stepped on the accelerator, and we chugged down the alley on the way to the convent with about twenty School Sisters of Notre Dame in full dress uniform waiting to hear me mumble the Suscipiat.

When we arrived at the convent, Pa said he'd wait for me. "Do the engine good to warm up, and the heater's goin' good now." I didn't try to talk him out of it, because I knew Pa liked to sit in that car. Sometimes he'd go sit in that car for an hour or more, doing nothing. He felt safe in there, I guess. And maybe it made him feel like a man of means, owning his own car and all. Besides, it was starting to snow, and I had forgotten to wear my galoshes for the walk home.

I entered the convent by a side door and walked down a hallway to a door that opened into the small sacristy that had another door opening to the altar. The chapel could also be entered from the rear through the nuns' living room that was always open to the chapel. There were five pews along one wall and a narrow aisle to access them.

From the sacristy that morning, I could hear the steady hum of the nuns in their pews reciting the rosary. My mind picked up the even pacing and the melody of their voices, and I began a silent recitation with them. I stepped quietly to the door leading to the altar. It was open a crack, and I looked out at the pews with the nuns, heads bowed, folded hands moving rosary beads—not the five-decade rosaries you get assigned in the confessional for certain sins I won't reveal here, but the fifteen-decade rosary each wore on her belt at all times.

I looked at the altar, saw the candles already burning, and offered a short prayer of gratitude. Candle wicks have uncanny and mysterious powers for escaping the tapers of fourth-grade altar boys. The rest of the altar was dressed and decorated with red poinsettias.

"Merry Christmas, Richard." It was Father hustling into the sacristy from the hallway. "I'm glad you got a ride here. Too cold to walk."

"A ride, Father?"

"Yes, I saw your dad freezing his . . . well, freezing in your car out back."

"My dad?"

"I didn't know you were Smitty's boy."

"You know my dad, Father?"

"Of course. He's been delivering . . . well, delivering supplies to the rectory since he bought the tavern. Drops a case off at the convent now and then, too. I told him to get in here and watch his son serve Christmas mass, or I'd find a new supplier."

"But he ain't Catholic, Father."

"Neither was Jesus. Now let's get these good sisters their Christmas mass."

I guess I never felt so light and relieved and grateful in my entire boyhood. Father and probably all of the sisters knew I was only half-Catholic, and it didn't matter. And they all knew Pa. And Pa was at the back of the chapel, watching me serve Christmas mass to all of the School Sisters of Notre Dame at Our Lady of Lourdes Parrish in full dress uniform.

When I held the paten under their chins, I knew Pa was wondering what the hell I was doing. The same when I rang the bells and poured water and wine into the priest's chalice.

Oh, it was a proud and thankful moment for a fourth-grade boy. Proud because I didn't make any mistakes, and thankful because the sisters said the prayers at the foot of the altar with me; and with them carrying the load, I rattled off the Suscipiat without a hitch.

Pa had the Ford running and warmed up when I crawled into the car after the mass. Before he put the shift lever into first gear, he said, "That was somethin', Son. Somethin' I never saw before. Where'd you learn to do all that?" I don't think he expected an answer, and it's a good thing because I was grinning too hard to answer.

When we got to the side street leading to the alley behind Smitty's Bar, Pa drove past it.

"Where we goin', Pa?"

"Let's take a little ride before we go home."

"But it's still dark."

"I know the way, light or dark."

We drove halfway to Peshtigo to Roland Schmedley's farm. Roland was one of Pa's Lutheran customers. The lights were on in the house and in the barn.

"I figured they'd be milkin'." Pa said, "Come along." I followed Pa into the barn. Roland and his three sons were indeed milking the herd of Holsteins. We all said, "Merry Christmas" and commented on the cold outside.

"Cows keep the barn warm," Roland said with a thick German accent. Then he led us to a stanchion with no cow in it. "Pick out any one you want," Roland offered. I looked into the stanchion. On the floor, lying on a bed of clean straw were Roland's hunting dog, Emma, and five beagle pups, all nuzzling their mother's belly.

"Looks like Old Whiskers left your Christmas present here, Son," Pa said, grinning like I'd never seen him grin before.

One of the pups looked up at me, and I grabbed it before someone said, "Wake up, Richard. You're dreaming." So when we got home to Ma that Christmas morning, I was a half-Catholic boy with a Lutheran dog and a firm belief in miracles.

# *Christmas is Coming and So Are We!*

Many of us who spent our pre-retirement lives in cold climates had a post-retirement dream. It looked something like this:

"Honey, let's sell the big house and all the stuff we don't need. We can downsize, buy a condo down south, and spend our old age relaxing in sunshine and balmy breezes."

"But, dear, what about our family here? Won't we miss our children and grandchildren? And what about Christmas?"

"Listen, honey. You can bet they'll want to come visit us, get out of that cold and snow. Christmas in Florida for all of us! Doesn't that sound great?"

"It does. The kids seem excited to get out of the cold... Oops, there goes the computer again. More e-mails."

❄ ❄ ❄

## You've Got Mail!

*From: Little Sister Mandy in Runny Nose, MN*
*November 6, '99@aol.com*

*Hi Moms and Pops,*

*So there you two are in your new Florida condo like all retired, relaxed and warm.*
*Honestly, totally GREAT! Lucky you.*
*Little Ezra says, "Miss you." Honestly, his first-grade teacher is such a grump. She got all bent because he bit some other kid. Like, I mean, where did he learn that if not in school? I just told her she should make the other kids set better examples. Then Big Ezra's mom told me he bit every kid and half the dogs in town until he was in fifth grade. So it must be in the genes or something. The school will just have to wait for Little Ezra to outgrow it. Honestly, Big Ezra never bites anybody anymore.*
*Hey, how about Christmas? I mean, like how will we all survive not being together for Christmas? Honestly, I hate to think about it. Big Ezra says you should invite us all down there. Him and his big ideas! Honestly.*
*I suppose we could bring sleeping bags. With Barbie, Joe and their twins, and Charlie, Rose and Aesop, that would only be ten—and you two. Well, anyway, like think about it. I mean it could work out, you know? You do have two bedrooms and two bathrooms. And we are family.*
*Big Ezra says his Christmas present to Daddy would be some advice on how to manage his 401-K (whatever that is) now that he's retired and has all that money. Honestly, Big Ezra is soooo smart about business stuff. He says just don't take any advice from Joe. Big Ezra says Joe can't even manage his kids. I don't know why Barbie married him anyway. Honestly, all he ever gave her was hyperactive twins.*

*Gotta go!*
*Think about Christmas*
*Little Ezra sends xxxx. Me too!*
*I'll e-mail the others about Christmas*

❄ ❄ ❄

## You've Got Mail!

*From: Big Sister Barbie in Fourwheel Drive, MN
November 7, '99 @aol.com*

Dear Mama and Daddy,

What's this about you two hosting Christmas in Florida? GREAT IDEA! (Even if it was Big Ezra's.) The twins can't wait for Popo to take them to see Mickey and Shamu (like you promised you would, Daddy). Maybe you could take Aesop and Little Ezra too and give us stressed-out, UNRETIRED parents a day (or two—hint, hint) at the beach without kids.

Joe and I are totally, I mean TOTALLY exhausted. Even their Ritalin doesn't slow down Hans and Fritz. They'll probably drown Mandy's and Charlie's kids in your pool.

Daddy, Joe says not to take any financial advice from Big Ezra. Joe says Big Ezra doesn't know his . . . from the S&P 500 (whatever that is). Why did Mandy marry him, anyway? Joe says there's big money to be made in office buildings in Escanaba, Michigan. And he knows a guy who can get you in on the ground floor. Joe says your money would be safer than in U.S. treasuries. He'll explain it all to you Christmas.

Whoops! Gotta run. Hans and Fritz kidnapped the neighbor's cat again and are giving it a haircut in the kitchen. Uh-oh, I hear a dog in there, too. Always something! More later.

Later: The cat looks pretty bad. Think about putting Friskers in a kennel while we're there for Christmas.

Love always,

Barbie

❄ ❄ ❄

## You've Got Mail!

*From: Charlie Boy in Capnmittens, MN*
*November 8, '99 @Juno.com*

*Hey there, Folks,*

*Never thought my own parents would leave their only son freezing in Minnesota while they're living it up in a new condo in sunny Florida. Me and Rose can hardly wait for our turn to retire, and that's the truth.*

*Just clicked on an e-mail from Mandy. You sure you want us all there for Christmas? Sounds like fun to me and Rose. Rose says not to worry about the cooking. She'll take care of it all. You know Rose and her fancy meals.*

*I promised Aesop that me and him would bust a gut eating those good old Florida shrimp. Buy a load of jumbos before we get there, Mom, and I'll pay you back.*

*Hey, Dad, nothing goes better with shrimp than a cold beer, right? Lay in a good supply of Bud for me and you. And get some of that fancy-schmancy microbrew for Rose. You know Rose! I'll pay you back.*

*Rose just yelled no kitchen cleanup for her if she's doing all the cooking. Mandy and Barbie can do the dishes, right, Mom?*

*Aesop wants to know if your pool's got a diving board. He wants to show Grams and Gramps his famous cannonballs. Better warn your neighbors. Santa promised him a surfboard and scuba gear to try out in his rich grandparent's pool. Maybe you could buy it for him down there so we don't have to haul it down on the plane. Try to get a deal, right, Dad? I'll pay you back.*

*And, Mom. Could you pick up a Christmas present for me to give Rose? You know what a klutz I am about shopping. I think I still owe you two a present from last year. Try to stay under twenty-five bucks, but get something that looks like it cost a lot more. You know Rose. I'll pay you back.*

*See ya'll soon. Can't wait. Rose and Aesop neither.*

*Brother Charlie Boy*
*P.S. Don't forget them shrimp.*

❄ ❄ ❄

## You've Got Mail!

*From: Little Sister Mandy in Runny Nose, MN.
November 9, '99 @aol.com*

*Hi again, Moms and Pops (A.K.A. Grandma and Grandpa Claus),*

*I guess I really got the ball rolling, huh? Everybody's going to Florida for Christmas. Honestly, I mean beyond COOL, like TOTALLY AWESOME!*

*No work for you two though. We kids will do everything. I'll do the cooking, Mom. Except would you do your pot roast and baked beans, and maybe your seven layer salad? I mean, who could even try to do those like you do? Honestly. And Big Ezra says it wouldn't be Christmas if you didn't bake a Kringle for breakfast and your GREAT EGGS BENEDICT. Thanks, Mom.*

*I'll cook everything else, and Barbie can help. And Rose can clean up the kitchen. She should do her share too, right, Mom?*

*One more thing. Big Ezra wants Little Ezra to have a REAL Christmas tree like he had when he was little. Big Ezra is sooo romantic. He says a blue spruce with lots of pine cones might be a little hard to find in Florida, but if you really shop around, he's sure you can find one, even if it is a little expensive. And get a real tall, bushy one.*

*Be sure to send Santa a map to your condo. Little Ezra still believes! Big Ezra's mom said he believed until fifth grade. Isn't that great? Honestly, even if he did get teased a lot.*

*Pops, Big Ezra says not to touch any ideas about your money Joe gives you with a ten-foot blue spruce. Get it?*

*Luv, Luv, Luv,*

*Me, Little Ezra, Big Ezra, Mandy*

❄ ❄ ❄

## You've Got Mail!

*From: Rose, Capnmittens, MN*
*November 10, '99 @Juno.com*

*Dear Liz and Ed:*

*Just a quick message re: Xmas. Charlie is really excited even though our tickets are costing a fortune and flying always gives me a migraine. I'll probably spend Xmas in bed. Could Charlie and I have your bedroom if the migraine is a bad one?*

*But no matter how sick I am, count on me to do the cooking. I've got some new recipes I'm drying to try, Mexican and Middle East cuisine. I'll send you a list of the ingredients I'll need. You can probably find most of it at Albertsons or Publix. Otherwise, you may have to try some of those specialty stores in Tampa.*

*Keep your fingers crossed. Charlie and Aesop always get the flu for Christmas. Be sure to get your shots. If Charlie and Aesop are coughing, sneezing, and throwing up, and I have a terrible migraine, we should for sure have your bedroom, don't you think? I mean, to protect the others.*

*Bye, Rose*

❄ ❄ ❄

## You've Got Mail!

*From: Big Sister Barbie in Fourwheel Drive, MN*
*November 10, '99 @aol.com*

*Hi, Mama and Daddy,*

Can't wait for Christmas. Really, the twins are extra excited, even full of the extra dose of Ritalin their pediatrician prescribed. She said she'd take them off for their Christmas vacation, so prepare yourselves. They want Popo to take them and their cousins to Magic Kingdom, Epcot, Sea World, MGM, Universal, and Busch Gardens (they hear the other kids tell about the places in Florida their grandparents take them). But I said they had to choose three.

By the way, Mama, Mandy and Rose both think they're doing the cooking. Joe says if Rose cooks, we'll all get the you-know-whats from that you-know-what she calls "Goor-May." Mama, why don't you just tell Rose it's your kitchen, and Mandy is your daughter? Joe says blood is thicker than water, and you wouldn't let him or Big Ezra do the cooking, would you? Daddy, you're on the condo board, aren't you? Just tell Rose there are rules against exotic cooking smells. Anyway I thought you should know before we all get down there and the you-know-what hits the fan.

More news: Joe told Hans and Fritz there's no Santa Claus, and they told every kid in their class. The teacher really got fumed because a lot of the kids were crying and like hysterical, and their parents had to leave work to take them home. Joe says it's about time they all got a good dose of reality. He is so practical. But you better warn Mandy. You know how nutty she and Big Ezra are about Santa Claus and Little Ezra. Joe says Big Ezra still believes in the Easter Bunny, so don't put any investment eggs in his basket. Get it?

More later, I'm on my way to the doctor.

Later: Just got home from Dr. Katzenjammer. Guess what? No Popo's Egg Nog Specials for me this Christmas. I'm pregnant, and it looks like twins again.

*Mama, could you keep Hans and Fritz for a couple weeks after Christmas so Joe and I can have some "alone" time? You know, before I get too big. I called their teacher, and she says not to worry about missing school. She said to take the rest of the year if we need it.*

*Christmas can't come too soon for us.*

*Barbie*

❄ ❄ ❄

## You've Got Mail!

*From: Brother Charlie Boy in Capnmittens, MN*
*November 11, '99 @aol.com*

*Hey, Folks, How ya'll doin'?*

*I had a helluva time getting plane tickets, but I lucked out. GREAT DEAL!*

*Flights into Sarasota and Tampa were pretty expensive, so I booked us on a Disneyworld charter (pretty shrewd, huh?).*

*We get into Orlando at midnight on the 24$^{th}$. With the tickets and all, I couldn't afford to rent a car, but like I told Rose, you'd want to pick us up anyway in the big, new Lincoln you bought. Besides, I figured you'd be looking for an excuse to get away from Barbie's twins. Right, Dad? Better get there a little early. You know how Rose is about airports, especially with a migraine. And me and Aesop will probably have the flu. Don't worry about driving back from the airport, Dad. I'll pilot that baby. We'll open the new Lincoln up and let 'er whistle Dixie, right, Dad?*

*Hey, darned nice of you to take all four of the kids to the parks for two days. Just heard from Barbie. Kinda keep an eye on Aesop, though. He throws up easy on some of them rides, especially if he's got the flu. Remember how I always threw up easy, Dad?*

*What a super Christmas we're going to have. You two can just sit back, take it easy, and enjoy it all. You shouda retired and moved to Florida years ago.*

*Charlie Boy*
*P.S. Got them shrimp yet?*
*Remind me to pay you back.*

❄ ❄ ❄

## BRADENTON HERALD

Monday, November 12, 1999
Classified
Condos/Villas
For Sale: Almost-never-lived-in 2BR, 2BA condo fully furnished. Owners must sell before Dec. 25. Family situation requires quick move!
Make an offer!

# *A Christmas Secret*

*Pssst.* I mentioned this to Bob and Carol, Pete and Sally, Ron and Louise, and maybe a few others. But let's keep this between you and me: I heard Santa Claus isn't coming to town anymore

PEOPLE WHO TELL me a secret should also tell me how many other people they have told. Sometimes I try to tell a secret I was told, but can't find anyone who hasn't heard it. There may be some people who promise never to tell and never do. But not many. I have a head full of secrets from people who promised never to tell them to anybody, but told them to me. Furthermore, they made me promise never to tell anyone else. I promised, but told them anyway. It seems that secrets are easier to tell than to keep. That's just human nature.

That said, I am about to reveal a secret. One I have kept for more years than I can remember. My generation may criticize me for revealing it now, but after much thought I am going to, as the saying goes, come clean. It is time for the generation becoming grandparents to know the secret their parents have kept from them for, as I said earlier, I don't remember how many years.

Although I am not certain as to the when of what happened, I do remember clearly what did happen—one Christmas Eve Santa Claus didn't show up. Plainly and simply put, he made no appearance whatsoever. No explanatory note, no sign of having tried to get here, but couldn't make it. Just a no-show. No warning, no apology. It had never happened before. Pick any letter of the alphabet, c, for example, and you can find words beginning with that letter to describe the panic that ensued that Christmas morning: concern, confusion, consternation, chaos.

Nobody could figure out just what the devil was going on. It was a real shocker. A lot like the 1906 San Francisco earthquake, only worse. Covered the whole country, rich and poor, Catholics and Protestants, Democrats and Republicans, blacks, browns, whites . . . Didn't matter. Santa just damn well didn't stop anywhere. Over, done, and out! Period. Maybe in other countries, too. News didn't travel much beyond the borders of a country back then. Could have been worldwide.

What to do? Trusting and expectant folks had paid to have their chimneys cleaned for nothing, stuck their stockings on fireplaces, left room under their Christmas trees for presents, left milk and cookies on kitchen tables for . . . zip, zero, zilch. The jolly old man with white whiskers, a red suit, and a sack of presents slung over his shoulder was AWOL. Nobody knew what to think, let alone what to do.

Kids were in their beds waiting for dads to light their Christmas trees and call, "Santa's been here!" But Santa had not been. No trace of him. Trees were untrimmed, stockings on fireplaces hung limp and empty, floors under the trees were bare. And the excited kiddies upstairs with visions of sugarplums dancing in their heads were about to hear the music stop and to lose their faith in Christmas. Something had to be done. Parents had to act fast.

It's hard to know all that transpired just before sunrise that Christmas morning. Some remembered neighbors running from house to house, sounding the alarm to "keep the kids in bed!" Others give credit to party line telephones for spreading the word to four families with one call. Still others say all mothers sensed instinctively something amiss downstairs and kept their kids in bed. Whatever the reason, or reasons, no kid left the bedroom that Christmas morning until an excuse for Santa's inexcusable behavior had been fabricated and an alternative plan for celebrating the holiday had been hatched.

> "Santa's got the flu, and he wants us to spend
> the day playing the games he left last year."

"Santa's sleigh got caught in a blizzard when leaving the North Pole. He wants us to go to church and pray for better weather next year."
"The reindeer took a wrong turn, and the boys and girls on Mars got your toys."
"Stop blubbering and think of all the Jewish kids. They never get Christmas presents."

And so it went from family to family until that Christmas Day slid into the past, and the painful memory of the day receded from the consciousness of those innocent children whose own innocent children are now giving birth to equally innocent children. And so it goes.

The day passed and faded into history, as would the children's memories of the Christmas Kris Kringle passed them by. No lasting harm done that year. However, there was no guarantee Santa would resume normal operations the following year. What if he had developed a problem with alcohol and suffered eggnog hangovers? What if he were having marital problems? No one knew much about Mrs. Claus. What if the unthinkable had occurred: what if Santa Claus had died?

Speculation fueled more speculation until the mayor of a small town in southern Illinois put it all in perspective when he declared to the town council that, "Christmas just isn't Christmas without Santa Claus." An alderman at that meeting was so impressed by the mayor's perceptiveness and succinct summation of the situation that he put the mayor's words into a motion: "I move that Christmas just isn't Christmas without Santa Claus." Another alderman seconded the motion, there was a short discussion, and the motion passed unanimously. The following day, the minutes of that meeting were published in *The Trumpeter*, the local newspaper, on a page safe from the eyes of the children who read only the comics, or as most readers called them then, the "funnies."

It just so happened that several days after the publication of those minutes in *The Trumpeter,* the editor of *National Geographic* was scanning small-town newspapers in search of a locale for a future story, when he spotted those minutes tucked discreetly away from the funnies. It also just so happened that my cousin, Arvin, was at that time a crack reporter for *National Geographic* and well known for some pretty racy articles about aborigines in out-of-the-way places doing out-of-the-way things, with pictures and all.

So Arvin, my cousin, was summoned to the office of the editor of *National Geographic*.

"Arvin, we got to find out what the hell is up with Santa Claus. This damn dereliction of duty could give our kids the idea there ain't no Santa Claus at all. Think what would happen if this hit the fan. Raise up a nation full of cynics, nonbelievers. Banks being robbed, blood running deep in the streets. Let's face it, Arvin, Christmas just isn't Christmas without Santa Claus. You get your ass to the North Pole and find out what the hell that jolly old elf is up to."

In no time at all my cousin, Arvin, was pushing the doorbell on the front door of Mr. and Mrs. Claus. And because of his many experiences with the unusual, he was not taken aback when the door was opened by an elderly three-foot elf wearing a green and red pinafore. Now Arvin is a very tall fellow, and his greeter nearly fell over backward taking his measure. After a few pleasantries she agreed to grant him an audience with her husband. Accordingly, she escorted my cousin through the house and out the back door to a small, red building with a Santa Claus nameplate on the door. When he stepped inside, Arvin found himself face to white beard with the culprit in full uniform.

I suppose most reporters would be overcome with emotion at meeting Santa, but Arvin was accustomed to interviewing even stranger folk in stranger dress. So he got right down to business.

"Mr. Claus," he began, "you caused a helluva stir in the United States of America by forgetting to drop by Christmas Eve."

"Oh, I didn't forget."

"Then what happened? We depend on you to provide our Christmas. Our children expect you to be there for them."

"Is that so?"

Arvin detected a frosty tone to Santa's question. So to ease any tension that might be building, he injected a bit of levity into the interview. "To all of us in America Christmas just isn't Christmas without Santa Claus." Then he added, pointing to a bank of snow outside the picture window, "If you get my drift."

Santa smiled and looked my cousin straight in the eye. "Now let me give you my drift, Mr. smarty-pants *National Geographic* reporter. I've seen some of your articles, and I suspect I may be the only fully-clothed subject you have interviewed." This insightful observation took Arvin by surprise and prompted his next probe.

"*Touché*, Santa. Why don't you just tell me your story?" And, having said that, he took out his notebook and settled into a chair with carved reindeer-antler arms.

Santa accepted the invitation and began. "For starters, I am old and tired. The last time I tried to sling that big sack over my shoulder, I damn near collapsed. And the arthritis in my fingers hurts like hell every time I slap the reins to get Dasher, Dancer, Prancer, Vixen, Cupid, Comet, Donder and Blitzen off their butts. They're getting old, too, you know?"

Being a young man at the time and not yet suffering from arthritis, Arvin obviously did not know; but he nodded in assent.

Santa continued, "I am not immortal. Nobody and nothing hang around forever. And furthermore, I am not a jolly old philanthropist who gets a kick out of stuffing oranges and walnuts into stockings hanging on fireplaces. Do I enjoy sliding down sooty old chimneys?" Santa paused. "You ever try that, Mister hot-shot *National Geographic* reporter?" Arvin shook his head and made an entry in his notebook.

Then Santa got directly to the point of his dissertation. "I am a teacher, Arvin. And every teacher's ultimate objective is to turn the classroom over to his students when his teaching days are over. Mine are over, but what I taught is still there. Your turn, my boy. Pick it up and run with it." Arvin looked perplexed.

Santa rose from his La-Z-Boy and pointed an arthritic index finger at his interviewer. "I said, 'Your turn, my boy.' Time for you to teach the spirit of Christmas as I have taught it to you. Do you get my drift?" And he gazed out the window Arvin had pointed to only minutes earlier. "Now I will level with you, Arvin. This whole gift-giving lesson I taught has been more fun for me than for you and your offspring. It really is more fun to give than to receive. And your generation will discover that when you start buying all those doll buggies, toy pistols, and Parcheesi games for your kids yourselves."

Arvin interrupted, "But how . . . ? Where . . . ?"

Santa stopped him in mid-question. "You can damn well betcha you'll get all the help you need from toy manufacturers, department stores, and specialty shops. They'll smell a tasty piece of cheese when you put it under their noses. My elves are old, too—you met Mrs. Claus. And the roof on my workshop leaks like hell every spring. I plan to find the young elves jobs at racetracks and pension off the old ones. I have already offered to sell my workshop and warehouse to Wal-Mart. Made an offer on a condo in Florida."

"But what about our children?" My cousin thought he might be able to convince Santa to stick around for a few more years.

"Oh, don't worry about your children. You can fool them into believing I'm still on duty. Telling a little white lie is a helluva lot easier than keeping a secret. And when they're old enough to know better, they'll be on their way to playing Santa Claus for their own children. You see, son, our teachers leave us, but what they have taught continues to live if their students have been taught well. Go on home, my boy, and prove to Old Santa I have taught you well. Get my drift?"

Arvin did go home. And he wrote an article about the North Pole. But not until the last page did he write about his interview with Santa. He knew his secret would be safe because no one ever got to the last page of a *National Geographic* article, including the editor.

Instead, Arvin spread the word in an each-one-tell-one chain of communication. So that by the following Christmas Santa's legacy was fulfilled. Amazing what Americans can do when they put their minds to it.

Before my cousin died, he gave me the notebook in which he had recorded his interview with Santa Claus. I kept that secret all these years. But now my generation is getting old. Like Santa, we have arthritic fingers, weak hearts, and other ailments. And if we have been good teachers, our children will be Santa to us in our old age, as we were to them in their childhood. And their children will do the same for them. For if there is one thing we know, it is that life is a circle.

# *A Little Christmas Magic*

ON VARIOUS STAGES he had been Ebenezer Scrooge, Jacob Marley, and all three of Dickens' ghosts. Now, as Purdy walked past the Christmas tree and the piano in the commons area of Northland Acres Retirement Village, right in the middle of Adolph Schmeling's old cornfield, he whispered his favorite line from the character he had never played, "God bless us . . . everyone."

❄ ❄ ❄

Purdy Boville was born Christmas Eve in the year 1930. The small hospital in northeastern Wisconsin where he was born had never before registered "Purdy" as a birth name, and the nurse who wrote it on the certificate had to ask for the spelling. "The same like he looks," the young mother answered in the dialect of the region. "Ain't he purdy as a pitcher though?" And the nurse, not wanting to saddle a boy who weighed ten pounds at birth with the name Pretty, wrote down *Purdy Boville*. Father's Name: *Leopold*. Mother's Name: *Mary Louise*. Race: *White*. Religion: *Catholic*. And so his life began.

Mary Louise delighted in Purdy's Christmas Eve birth and declared to all who admired him that he was the best Christmas present ever. Leo was less enthusiastic. He was eighteen, a bridegroom of six months, and doing odd jobs while waiting for something to open at the paper mill. Those were the depression years, and a baby to feed was, well, a baby to feed. Purdy's hungry gulps soon depleted Mary Louise's meager supply of mother's milk, and Leo had to buy cartons of Carnation evaporated milk from the corner grocer on credit. Purdy was the only baby Doc Wimmer ever delivered who never lost any of his birth weight. "A strapping boy, Mrs. Boville," he described the "pitcher of health" on his examining table. "Gonna eat you outta house and home. How's Leo's nervous stomach?"

Now seventy-two years old, Purdy lay on his father's bed, comparing its regular size to that of the king size in his small apartment near the theater district in Manhattan. It was Christmas Eve and another birthday. Leaving his sixties had been a difficult passage, and three birthdays later, he still thought of himself as a much younger man than he was. The passage of time mystified him. "When you get old, the clock speeds up," Leo once told him. Purdy's personal metaphor was that life is like riding his sled down Swanson's hill used to be. The closer he got to the bottom, the faster he went.

After graduating from high school, Purdy disappointed his parents and dismayed the foreman of the pulp mill by turning down an offer to work on the log piles ". . . until something better opens up. Follow in your dad's tracks." Bert Madden offered, "A year or two on the logs should be just the ticket for a big fella like you."

Instead, at his English teacher's urging, Purdy went off to college to become a teacher. To pay his expenses, he took a job assisting the college janitors, doing just about anything that needed doing, especially the heavy work. The drama director discovered him moving stage equipment and, needing a big man for the role of Jean Valjean in *Les Miserables,* auditioned him. Purdy played the part, received high praise, changed his major to drama, and married the stage. He went from little theater to bigger theater to Broadway, with some movie and television work along the way. And now, on his seventy-second birthday, he was about to play a role he had never played before, on an unfamiliar stage, for an audience he wanted very much to please. He was nervous and shifted his position on Leo's too-small bed.

". . . a beautiful sight, we're happy tonight, walkin' in a winter wonderland." The music came from the living room where Andy Williams was singing carols from the Bose radio and CD player Purdy had given Leo on his eighty-ninth birthday. Leo wanted the player on a small table next to his La-Z-Boy recliner. Purdy had explained the stereo effect would be better from across the room, but Leo insisted a radio belongs next to a chair. The Andy Williams *Merry Christmas* CD was also a gift from Purdy, and he suspected the CD player had not been used before.

". . . In the meadow we will build a snowman. . ." A lot of memories in that song. He had never married, but he had come close a few times. The theater was wife enough for him.

". . . and pretend that he is Parson Brown." Just for fun, Purdy listened through the music for the thump of Santa's sleigh on the roof as he had done as a boy, trying to recapture the childhood magic of Christmas.

The magic of Christmas. That's what Christmas was, magic.

Purdy opened his file of Christmas memories and selected one from his fourth birthday. There he was, lying in bed trying to fall asleep so Santa could come. He remembered the slow grind of the weeks, days, and hours before Christmas mornings. "Backward, turn backward, O Time in your flight, Make me a child just for tonight."

❄ ❄ ❄

"Mama, make the twins shut up. They're carryin' on in their room, and I can't sleep." Peggy and Billy were three and shared the bedroom next to Purdy's. Then suddenly it was morning. He had slept. Santa had come and gone.

The three children were not allowed to see the tree until Leo turned the lights on and shouted to their trembling bodies in the half-light, "He's been here!" Only then could they dash for their treasures arranged in three neat piles under the tree.

"Remember," Mary Louise always cued them, "Purdy's are wrapped in red, Billy's in green, and Peggy, honey, yours are in the white tissue paper."

He remembered there were few surprises in the gifts under the Boville tree. The guidelines for preparing children to take their places in the adult world had been in place for many generations. Boys were headed for the mill, girls for marriage.

So every Christmas morning, Peggy tore white tissue paper off a new Sunday-go-to-church dress, a doll, hair ribbons, underwear, and a refurbished doll buggy or garment Santa had mysteriously whisked away to his North Pole workshop weeks earlier. Purdy and Billy unwrapped new corduroy knickers, knee socks, long underwear, and a toy truck, six-shooter in a holster, or metal soldiers, toys the brothers were expected to share with each other. The family received oranges and chocolate-covered cherries in a box, as well as decks of playing cards and board games to replace the old ones that had been grimy and missing pieces since the previous New Year's Day.

When the kids started first grade at Saint Joseph's, new prayer books, rosaries, and Saint Christopher medals on neck chains, all blessed by Father Champlain, were added to their Christmas piles. "Your old ones was a disgrace to the church," Mary Louise proclaimed. "Santa seen that way up at the North Pole."

❄ ❄ ❄

His mother's words, as he remembered them, returned Purdy to 2002. He checked the time. Only a few minutes had passed, and Andy Williams was still singing, ". . .better not cry, Santa Claus is coming to town."

How real Santa Claus was to Purdy sixty-three years ago when he was in third grade at Saint Joe's. Santa was not held in high regard by The Teaching Sisters of Saint Francis. For three weeks before Christmas vacation, Sister Thomasina reminded her third graders several times daily that,"Christmas is to celebrate the coming of Jesus, not Santa Claus." She stopped short of denouncing the tradition in so many words, but she tried now and then to shake her students' faith in Santa. "How can it be," she asked the class one day, "that his whiskers don't burn off sliding down all those fiery chimneys?" Sister Thomasina had a way of exposing fraud.

The question seemed reasonable to Purdy and, therefore, disturbing. Sister had a point. How could a fat man with a white beard carrying presents wrapped in tissue paper slide down chimneys with black coal smoke headed in the other direction and keep his whiskers intact? Purdy's faith was being tested.

But Larry Burns saved the day. "I'll betcha he carries a big jug of water in his sleigh and waters 'em down." This explanation relieved the class, and Sister Thomasina resisted pressing the point by asking why it was that water in a jug didn't freeze in twenty-below-zero weather.

Purdy wondered whatever happened to Larry Burns. Probably followed in his dad's tracks and worked on the logs until something better opened up at the mill.

*Dads*, Purdy thought, *are probably more responsible for perpetuating the Santa Claus myth than mothers*. At least that was true in his family. It was Leo, not Mary Louise, who loved the magic of Christmas as much as the kids did. Purdy remembered a conversation he and his dad had in the kitchen several days before Christmas.

*"We gonna leave him milk and cookies like the other kids, Dad?"*

*"Don't you think he must get awful sick of the same old milk and cookies all the time?"*

*"Ain't we gonna leave him nothin', Dad?"*

*"Sure. But we always leave him somethin' a little different."*

*"A little different, Dad?"*

*"Sure. Somethin' he don't get so much of, like he does milk and cookies."*

*"Like what, Dad?"*

*"Well, son, when your old dad comes home from the mill all tired out from workin' the night shift, what's the first thing he goes for?"*

Purdy recalled searching his mind for the answer to Leo's question, then the flush of embarrassment he felt when he found it.

"Oh, Dad! Please, Dad. Dad, you can't mean . . . not a cold beer!"

"Bingo! Nothin' goes better when you're hot and tired from

slidin' down chimneys than a cold beer . . . and a pickled Polish sausage!"

"But Santa don't drink beer and eat pickled Polish sausages!"

"He does at our house."

"How do you know, Dad?"

"I set 'em out Christmas Eve and they're always gone Christmas morning."

And they always were.

". . . It came upon a midnight clear, that glorious song of old . . ." The music removed that particular Christmas ghost from Purdy's reveries. Maybe he should get his clothes changed. Again, he looked at his watch. Still plenty of time. "Time," he said aloud, "that thief of life." Peggy and Billy were gone now, and Mary Louise. Did they and all those Christmases really happen, or were they dreams? Perhaps they were all still here. Of course they were. He couldn't shake them from his head if he tried. Peggy and Billy and Mama; the big, decorated spruce in the corner of the living room; Sister Thomasina; the wrapped packages he opened expectantly, already knowing what was in them; The Lone Ranger, Our Gang, Charlie Chan, Fibber McGee and Molly, George and Gracie, Eddie Cantor and Harry Vonzel. All still here, and all a part of him. *Nothing's ever really gone,* he reasoned. *As long as I am here, they will be with me.*

Andy Williams was still with him also, ". . . how still we see thee lie. Above thy deep and dreamless sleep . . ." Purdy rose from the bed, stepped to the small closet, opened the folding doors, and peered inside, visually checking off the items he would soon need. Satisfied, he returned to Leo's bed.

". . . the hopes and fears of all the years . . ." When did his maturing mind force him to move Sana Claus from the real to the make believe? He thought back and replayed a scene from third grade.

❄ ❄ ❄

A small group of "Saint Josephites" huddled together for warmth on the school playground—recess, he supposed. They were hunched into their mackinaws and neck scarves to shield themselves from the December weather. From their chatter through steamy puffs of breath, a serious issue emerged. What is Santa's motivation for being so nice to kids who, as the nuns often reminded them, were riddled with imperfection and well-advised to make frequent acts of contrition, as well as weekly visits to Father Champlain's confessional?

Punky Rastall thought Santa Claus was a millionaire and just liked spending money on kids, whether they were good or not. Nobody, Punky claimed, ever got a piece of coal in his stocking, or, as his father had changed the threat to make it more fearful, a "horse's apple." Petey Peterson begged to differ. He was certain some kid somewhere, at some time, had found something rotten in his stocking—maybe no girl had, but a boy for sure.

Becky Brown said it was just like the Easter Bunny. "Some of God's creatures are a lot like angels, only they have reindeer instead of wings." Ronald Smith said she was nuts, because only a nut would believe in the Easter Bunny. That remark made Becky cry, and she stomped away to tell Sister Mary Rose.

Allen Remington figured Santa was a lot like nuns. "They don't get paid like the publics do." Finally, the consensus was that Santa did it for the milk and cookies he got at every house. "He really likes eatin' cookies and dippin' 'em in milk. That's why he's so fat," Bobby Schneider concluded, a conclusion that made Purdy uneasy.

Suppose his father was wrong about Santa's tastes! What if Santa wasn't drinking the beer, but pouring it out in the sink? What if he was insulted by the Polish sausage, or he ate it and it made him sick? What if he would choose this year to get even and skip the Boville house altogether? These and other terrible possibilities raced through Purdy's mind. He would ask his dad to change their offering to the standard milk and cookies.

"I want to give him what the other kids do, Dad."

"Okay, son, if that's the way you want it. But I still say old Santa must get awful sick of all them milk and cookies."

"Thanks, Dad... Dad?"

"What, son?"

"How can Santa get to every house in the world in one night?"

"He just does, that's all."

"But, Dad, why?"

"Listen, Purdy, son. Sometimes there ain't no answers for the 'how' and 'why' questions you and me can dream up. Nobody knows for sure. But we can see the 'whats' that happen, and it's the 'whats' that count. It don't matter so much how or why Santa comes. We just know he does. And until you know for sure he don't, he'll be here every Christmas."

"Okay, Dad."

"Good. So milk and cookies it is. I'll keep the beer and sausage for myself."

Purdy knew then there was no Santa Claus.

❄ ❄ ❄

". . . May your days be merry and bright, and may all your Christmases be white."

Purdy's favorite carol drifted in from the living room, and he hummed along. It was the last selection on the Andy Williams disc. Purdy listened until the next disc dropped and Anne Murray opened with *Joy to the World*. Then he swung his long legs to the floor, walked past the still-open closet, through the living room, and to the door that opened to the hallway.

He opened the door and looked to the left and to the right. The hallway was empty, as he knew it would be. All the other doors opening to the hallway were closed and probably locked, protecting the contents of the small apartments from neighbors who had no use for them and had never stolen anything.

Purdy counted eight doors between Leo's apartment and the intersecting hallway leading to the dining room and commons area. He stepped into the hallway and listened. Edna Thompson was playing *Jingle Bells* on the old piano Purdy knew was next to the Christmas tree for tonight's program. Edna had been playing *Jingle Bells* forever, first as the public school's elementary music teacher, then as the music director for the Methodist Church, and now as the resident musician for Northland Acres Retirement Village, located in the middle of Adolph Schmeling's former cornfield. Time marches on!

*Jingle Bells* was the processional music for the fourth, fifth, and sixth grades carolers from Saint Joseph's Elementary School, the chorus Purdy had sung in six decades earlier. The carolers, Purdy had been informed, would sing for the assembled residents for thirty minutes, just enough time for his preparations.

He returned to the bedroom, transferred his trappings from the closet to the bed, and began his transformation. He was as nervous as he had been any time he waited backstage on Broadway. He was afflicted with what he and his fellow professional thespians termed "the dressing-room shakes." He licked the sweat from his upper lip and recognized the familiar salty taste.

First the wig, the beard, and the bushy white eyebrows, then the red suit and boots, and finally the floppy hat. Purdy moved quickly to face himself in the dresser mirror. A little lipstick, now some rouge on his cheeks. His hands were shaking. Just about ready. From habit he vocalized his cue and his opening line.

Returning the few steps to the closet, he retrieved the sack holding thirty-seven gifts, all purchased and wrapped in tissue paper by Saint Joseph's Altar Society. There were boxes of chocolate-covered cherries, jars of hand lotion, neck scarves, decks of playing cards, flannel shirts, ballpoint pens, socks, aprons, calendars, and other useful items.

Purdy prepared to lift the sack to his shoulder. Fortunately, he was a large and still-strong Santa. The sack found his shoulder easily and rested there comfortably. He carried it out of the bedroom, through the apartment door, and into the hallway he knew would be empty. There he lowered it to the floor and listened.

He could hear the children singing in the commons area, accompanied by Edna Thompson. ". . . joyful and triumphant, O come ye, O come ye to Bethlehem." Purdy had been given the program in advance. The final carol, *Silent Night,* would be next. Then the recessional, *Jingle Bells,* applause from the appreciative audience, a moment or two for Edna to rub some flexibility into her arthritic fingers, and then his cue. Purdy lifted the sack again and walked gingerly to the intersecting hallway. His nervousness had been replaced with excitement and anticipation.

As he passed the closed apartment doors, he mentally visualized what was behind them. Each small apartment had its own special signature: antique vases filled with artificial flowers,

La-Z-Boys pulled close to television sets, a hand-knitted afghan over the back of a couch, a wall overloaded with family pictures, a dining table and chairs crammed into a too-small eating area, a floor lamp moved from the old farm house to the house in town and now here, in Adolph Schmeling's old cornfield. All stents keeping lifelines to the past open for the flow of memories.

At the intersection Purdy stopped and cleared his throat. The applause for the children was replaced by a murmur of voices. Then his cue: Leo's still-strong voice rising above those of his family of neighbors. "I hear someone coming." Quickly, Edna Thompson unleashed *"Here Comes Santa Claus,"* Purdy's cue, and Purdy sang out, "Ho, Ho, Ho!"

His "Ho, Ho, Ho," even from the distance he delivered it, was clearly audible in the commons area; and he sang out again, "Ho, Ho, Ho!" This gave life to Edna's fingers, and she thumped the piano keys with such feeling and exuberance that she might have been playing *The Star Spangled Banner, God Save the Queen* or *Onward Christian Soldiers*. Several in the audience had to adjust their hearing aids.

In he bounded, sack on his shoulder, still shouting, "Ho, Ho, Ho!" And Edna played louder still, ". . . right down Santa Claus Lane. . ." There was magic in her fingers, the magic of Christmas. And that same magic was in the eyes and ears and hearts of her listeners who had celebrated that magic for so many years.

Purdy looked his audience over as he lowered the sack from his shoulder, Edna's cue to stop the music. There was Curly Archambeau, now bald as a billiard ball; Marjorie Nettleton, once the best polka dancer in town, in her wheelchair; Chet Doyle, the town barber until his brain and tongue lost their harmony and he began taking gibberish to his customers; Bert Madden in plaid pants and a plaid shirt, still wondering why Purdy turned down his job offer; Emmaline Arthur, from the richest family in town, sitting right next to Henry Brickbauer, from the poorest. The great equalizer, age, had done its work.

And there, right in the middle of the celebrants was Leo Boville, as Mary Louise would have said, "grinnin' like a chessie cat." To have a son like Purdy was, well, somethin' special. And to share him with the Northland Acres family at Christmas was, well, somethin' very special indeed.

So Purdy played his role. He shook hands, he hugged, he told jokes, he shared memories, he handed out gifts wrapped in tissue paper, white for the ladies, colored for the gentlemen.

When he took Jenny Dishaw's hand to shake it, he did so gently to protect the brittle bones beneath her thin, white skin. He asked Bert Madden whatever became of Larry Burns and was told Larry, now retired, had risen to foreman of the pulp mill. "You coulda been there, too, boy," he was reminded.

Melrose Doran told him she had seen him in an old Western movie on channel 46. "Was I any good?" he asked.

"You was always a good boy, Purdy."

"No, I mean was I a good actor in that movie?"

"All you Boville kids was good. Never got in any trouble at all. Your ma and pa seen to that."

"Thank you, Mrs. Doran. Merry Christmas."

And so he moved from person to person in his disguise, but fooling no one as to his identity, thanks to Leo's inability to keep a secret. And when the party was over, he helped his dad back to his apartment.

❄ ❄ ❄

While Leo rested in his La-Z-Boy, Purdy went to the bedroom to change his clothes. When he returned to the living room, Leo was asleep. He thought about putting him to bed, but decided against it. Instead, he went to the refrigerator, took out a can of Budweiser and a pickled Polish sausage, and put them on the eating counter in the kitchen, next to the new sweater wrapped in red tissue paper he had bought at Macy's in "New York City."

He would sleep at the Comfort Inn and come back to say goodbye in the morning, Christmas morning. Then he would take a cab to Green Bay and catch a flight to New York, through Minneapolis.

Another birthday had come and gone. He was a year older and some wiser. The burden of growing older was somewhat compensated by growing wiser, he thought.

As a character in a play, Purdy had joked, "Old age is all in your head ... and your neck ... and your shoulders ... and hips ... and knees ... and ..." It was a good line and always brought a laugh. He knew he would feel the truth of it as he squeezed into his seat in the Northwest commuter plane tomorrow.

He walked down the corridor, past the closed doors of the "children" all nestled snug in their beds or La-Z-Boys. He hoped that sugar plums danced in their heads. He had given them a little Christmas magic one more time. And just as in the theater when a performer gives magic, the audience had returned it.

On various stages he had been Ebenezer Scrooge, Jacob Marley, and all three of Dickens' ghosts. Now as he walked past the Christmas tree and the piano in the commons area of Northland Acres Retirement Village, right in the middle of Adolph Schmeling's old cornfield, he whispered his favorite line from the character he had never played, "God bless us . . . everyone."

# Grandfather Liu's Christmas Gift

THE BRAINS OF old men are filled with stories, stories of triumph and stories of tragedy. Most they are eager to tell over and over. But some they keep locked deep inside their memory bank.

It took the key of Christmas to unlock Grandfather Liu's hidden memory.

❄ ❄ ❄

Xiang Liu left Beijing for America when he was twenty-two years old. A brilliant student, he had been recommended by his mathematics professors in China to the Department of Statistics at the University of Wisconsin, Madison. Xiang was awarded a teaching assistantship and a place in the graduate program. Although Xiang intended to return to China on the completion of his degree and assured his father he would, unforeseen persons and opportunities changed the direction of his life.

Xiang's first assignment at Wisconsin was to lead a discussion section for Introduction to Statistics. The course was filled with undergraduates for whom the language of statistics was as unfamiliar as was Xiang's native language. To his distress, Xiang soon discovered his English language teachers in Beijing had evaluated his ability to communicate in English much higher than did his American students. After his distorted attempts to answer students' questions about "measures of central tendency," a swarm of confused students buzzed into his office with more questions. Xiang tried again with minimal improvement. So the students, after checking and finding all other discussion sections for the required course filled, accepted their fates, as students must so often do.

Fortunately, one of the students in Xiang's section was Su Ming, who had an ear and a tongue for turning a Chinese-flavored pronunciation into an understandable English word. Her cue for "translation needed" was the simultaneous turning of thirty heads in her direction, whereupon she improved upon Xiang's rough approximations while Xiang nodded his head appreciatively. The students were amused by this "team teaching," which gave comic relief to an otherwise exasperating subject matter. Better yet, Xiang gave them all high grades for fear the ignorance displayed in their test booklets was the result of his inability to master English pronunciation and syntax and not their failure to learn statistics. Not one student from his section dropped the course after six-week exam grades were posted, a record for the Department of Statistics.

❄ ❄ ❄

Su Ming had lived in Madison all her life. After graduating from North High School, she attended the university off and on and worked in the restaurant owned and managed by her father, Henry, and her mother, Lilly. The restaurant was named The Dragon's Garden and was, depending on the travel experiences of the reviewer, reported to serve the most authentic Chinese food in Wisconsin, the USA, or possibly the whole world—and if not the most authentic, certainly the most. The Dragon's Garden was filled to capacity every noon for the all-you-can-eat buffet. Xiang ate there nearly every day, and when his eyes met Su Ming's as she cleared a table near his or restacked the buffet table, he blushed.

In time Xiang Liu finished his degree, improved his English, and was offered a post-doctoral fellowship in his department. By then, Henry Ming had died, and Lilly had turned the restaurant over to Su and returned to what family she had left in Beijing. And Xiang's shyness in the presence of Su had dissipated enough for him to propose in the old-fashioned American style, on one knee. Su corrected his pronunciation of "marry" and accepted. Xiang turned down the offer of a post-doc and went to work as the new owner-manager of The Dragon's Garden, where he made more money in three months than he would have in three years in the Department of Statistics.

Xiang and Su had a daughter, Li, and a son, Chan, whom they nicknamed Sam after Xiang's favorite symbol of American strength. Only one person was missing from Xiang's life. It was the man who had been both father and mother to him the first twenty-two years of his life. So again, Xiang wrote his father in Beijing, "Come to America, my father. You will find a good life here with my family which is also your family. And now you have a grandson who will benefit from your wisdom. We all want you here in America with us, Father."

To Xiang's surprise and delight, his father, after years of chewing on the decision and declining his son's invitations, wrote that he would come. To his neighbors and friends in Beijing, he announced that he was leaving for America. "An old man should be near his son," he proclaimed. Then he added, "And now his son's son." He excluded his son's wife and daughter because only sons were important in the Liu family tradition. Females, he believed, were decorative and useful, but not the strength of a family.

So Xiang flew from Madison to Chicago and then to Beijing on a United Airlines flight to fetch his father "home."

Weeks later, Su received a telephone call from Xiang in Beijing. Everything was in order there, and they would arrive in Madison the following week. "How are you managing with the children and the restaurant?" he asked. And did she miss him as much as he missed her? Su was greatly relieved by the call and assured her husband that all was well in Madison, and, yes, she did miss him and "Please hurry home."

❄ ❄ ❄

The following week, Su sat with Li and Sam in the waiting area for United Airlines flights from Chicago to Madison. She was happy her husband was almost home, yet apprehensive about the addition of her father-in-law to their household. He had never been to the United States, and she doubted he would find everything to his liking. By pre-arrangement, Grandfather Liu would care for the children, and Su would spend more time in the restaurant business. She and Xiang had discussed opening a Dragon's Garden II on the east side of town. She remembered Xiang once describing his father as a "pensive man with a shadow on his heart," an unusually poetic description for a statistician to make. How would such a man fit in?

Li was the first to see her father emerging from the plane, followed closely by an older carbon copy. The two paused, and Xiang peered into the assembled people peering back. Li tugged at her mother's skirt and pointed. "Go to them," Su told her, "and do as we practiced." On cue the girl ran to her father and grandfather and, in perfect Chinese dialect, greeted them.

"Welcome home, Father and Grandfather. Take my hand, Grandfather. We have been waiting a long time for you. Come and meet my mother and brother." It was a warm greeting by a precocious four-year-old. And Grandfather was astonished by this muffin who was the miniature in voice, movement, appearance, and spirit of her long-deceased grandmother. The resemblance was remarkable, and the old man's consternation did not go unnoticed by his daughter-in-law.

Grandfather Liu spoke only a little English when he landed at the Madison airport. Fortunately, Xiang and Su moved easily from one language to the other, and they had insisted that Li be bilingual as well. Sam, of course, still communicated in whoops and hollers, whines and sniffles. So Li took it upon herself to teach her grandfather English and was not only doing well with this endeavor, but was also endearing herself to him as they shared the household chores and the parenting of Sam.

After two months with the Xiang Liu family in America, Grandfather Liu concluded that Chan, or Sam as he was called, was unlikely ever to bring honor to the family. The boy was obstinate, resembled his mother, and showed none of the superior intelligence he remembered Xiang showing at that age. Li, on the other hand, was a piece of fruit worthy to grace any family tree. She was bright, beautiful, confident, and forthright. Her sensitivity to those around her was often in conflict with her penchant for speaking her mind. It was this contradiction in her grandmother that provoked the quarrel that once again tortured his dreams and ruptured his sleep. *If only there had been no sparks,* he thought. And then, *and no straw.*

As the bond between grandfather and granddaughter strengthened, so too did the memories he had repressed for years. The girl's likeness to Xiang's mother was eerie. He lay awake long hours every night replaying disquieting events from the past. Often he slept only to awaken at two or three o'clock in the morning, anxious and unsettled. "Why is it I can find no forgiveness for myself?" he fretted.

His father's unsettled state went unnoticed by Xiang. "We are now a happy family," he told Su. "We are together in America." She said nothing, but Su knew otherwise.

*The old man is not happy,* she thought. *There is a restless wind that inhabits his spirit, a bad dream from which he cannot awaken. He carries a burden. . . I wish I knew. . .*

The passage of time that so often heals had no effect on Grandfather's mood. His food, delivered from The Dragon's Garden, was not authentic Chinese as the locals believed. He missed his neighbors, his bed remained unfriendly to his aging body, and the natural commotion of a young American family was jarring to him. His son had neither time nor inclination to hear him talk of the "old days" in China, how the country was being corrupted by the government, and how the importation of Western ways was leading Chinese youth away from the teachings of Confucius. Most of all, Li, whom he loved dearly, was nonetheless a specter, a constant reminder of a psychological need for a forgiveness that could never be given.

❋ ❋ ❋

As winter shouldered autumn away, pieces of warm weather slipped away under each setting sun, and leaves with streaks and patches of orange, yellow, and red grew brittle and fell from their branches. The Christmas season was approaching, and Su was certain the spirit of Christmas would relieve her father-in-law's melancholy. She had been raised a Catholic by Henry and Lilly, and Li and Sam were baptized in that faith. Xiang had never embraced Christianity and long ago had forgotten most of the teachings of Confucius. He was neither a believer nor a non-believer, simply a questioner and non-joiner. Nonetheless, he agreed with Su that in America, Christmas was a time for celebration and always closed The Dragon's Garden Christmas Eve and Christmas Day, the only closures of the year.

Su loved all of the Christmas stories and songs, religious and non-religious. They all, she believed, contributed to the overall "Christmas Spirit," that intangible excitement in the air that generates anticipation, joy, tolerance, fellowship, and goodwill among people of all faiths.

Furthermore, she insisted that this spirit permeate the Liu household for a least a week before the big day itself. "You will not whine, not argue, not fight, not be disagreeable in any way, shape, or form. You will be nice to each other for one week . . . or else!" Even Sam got the message. Sadly, Grandfather did not.

If anything, Grandfather grew more sullen. Innocently, Li told him stories of Baby Jesus born in a manger, angels appearing to shepherds, wise men following a star to the infant, stories her mother had told her. In response he quoted sayings of Confucius, which were as incomprehensible to Li as her stories were to him. When she sang *Rudolf the Red-Nosed Reindeer* to him, he denounced the animal as a fabrication of Western capitalists. The bond between them was severely strained.

Quickly for Su and Xiang, but agonizingly slowly for the children, December 24th arrived. The restaurant was closed after the noon buffet, and Xiang and Su hurried home for their own holiday celebration. The tree, a tall and bushy spruce purchased at Brennan's Market on University Avenue, was trimmed and sparkled in one corner of the living room. The dinner table was dressed with a Christmas cloth and red and green candles. One gift for each child was under the tree. Santa would come that night, but Henry and Lilly had always given Su a "parents' present" Christmas Eve, and she continued the tradition with her own children.

❄ ❄ ❄

It was a warm, jolly evening with good food, plum wine, laughter, teasing, and presents, even a new robe for Grandfather, which he accepted graciously with apologies for not reciprocating with gifts of his own. Su noticed his mood lightening as the evening progressed. She was more than ever convinced of the power of the Spirit of Christmas to move people to higher planes of consciousness and empathy for one another. She was convinced that Charles Dickens must have known, rather than created, Ebeneezer Scrooge.

About ten o'clock Su offered to tidy the kitchen and living room for the arrival of Santa and shooed the others to their beds. They moved sleepily at her urging. When she was certain the children were entertaining visions of sugarplums, she placed their presents under the tree, one side for Li, the other for Sam. She wondered why they had bothered to christen him. Then she headed for bed in the dark, guided by Xiang's plum-wine snores.

As she neared the door to Grandfather's room, she saw his light was on. Buoyed by her personal Christmas spirit and perhaps the plum wine, she tapped on his door. Startled, Grandfather opened the door only enough to see Su. He hesitated, then opened the door wide enough for her to enter. She stepped to the small armchair next to the bed and sat. Then she pointed to his bed and motioned for Grandfather to sit also. He did.

Su look closely at the man whose face and posture were those of a man older than his actual years. He fingered a piece of jewelry, a necklace. There were tears on both cheeks, and his watery eyes were fixed on the necklace.

"This necklace . . . ," he began, "is missing a green bead. This necklace . . . a gift that gave misery instead of intended joy." He paused, head bent floorward, and his tears dropped upon his hands and the necklace. "Green jade embossed with gold, the only one of its kind on the necklace, strung as the centerpiece.

And with it went my peace and my love." One of his hands left the necklace and moved to cover his face. His shoulders hunched forward, and he sat silent.

"Tell me, Grandfather Liu," Su said softly. "Tell me. It is time to share your burden. Does not Confucius say that only through letting others help can a burden be lightened?"

Grandfather let his hand drop from his face back to the necklace. He fingered the necklace as a rosary might be fingered, one bead at a time. He raised his head, straightened his shoulders, and looked directly into the eyes of his daughter-in-law. And in her eyes he saw compassion and true caring. He dropped his defenses and at the same time his prejudice that only men could shape the history of a family. After a moment, he began to speak slowly and with an articulateness that revealed his story had been repeated to himself many times over many years.

"I was a young man, perhaps too young to take a wife whose temper was the equal of her beauty. Look at your daughter, Li, and see her loveliness. We were in love, filled with youthful passions, but lacking in experience and wisdom.

"We farmed a small piece of land owned by the government. Our profit was little, and most of it was returned for rent of our small plot and for use of the miserable quarters we were given to live in. We were poor, but no poorer than the factory workers in nearby Beijing. And our young love and dreams for a better future gave us happiness and hope.

"One day, returning from Beijing after having sold our vegetables at the market place, I was approached by a vendor who offered me this necklace for nearly all the money I had been paid for our crop. I thought it the most beautiful gift in all of China for the most beautiful wife in all of China. The vision of it around her lovely neck made me forget our poverty and the necessities for which the money was intended. So I bought the necklace with its many colored beads and presented it to her as a symbol of my love.

"She took it from me and in a fit of temper threw it back at me as the purchase of a fool who had spent money needed for the coming child. Angry words were exchanged, and in a like fit of temper, I left our home, vowing never to return.

"I went to Beijing, found work and stubbornly refused to return to our small farm. Such was the pride of a foolish young man."

At this point Grandfather handed the necklace to Su. She took it, looked at it closely, then handed it back to Grandfather, who continued.

"Neighbors brought word to me of her hardships, but my pride was unrelenting. Then a trusted friend sought me out and told me a child had been born, my son.

"The woman is very ill," he said. "You must go quickly, for the child's sake."

"Like lightning hitting my brain, I realized what misery my pride and arrogance had caused. On my bicycle I raced out of the city to the cottage I had raced away from months earlier. There I found our son, held by a neighbor. My wife was in our bed, asleep and breathing softly.

"I took the child and with him cradled in my arms went to the bed. She opened her eyes.

"And in those eyes there was no longer anger, only love; and she saw the same in mine. We professed our love, begged each other's forgiveness, and absolved each other for how stupidly we had behaved. Together, we named the child Xiang, and I laid him on the pillow next to her head. She gazed at our son lovingly and after a brief moment closed her eyes. She never opened them again, for a blood clot had broken loose and been carried to her heart. Xiang and I were left alone." He stopped.

Su was stunned and filled with compassion for the old man before her. She moved to his side and took his limp hand in hers. "The blood clot was not of your making. You raised a fine son who brings honor to your family. You had your wife's forgiveness. Why do you still torment yourself?"

"Because," Grandfather answered, "no man is truly forgiven until he forgives himself. As my love was being prepared for burial, I removed a green bead, gold-embossed, the only one of its kind on the necklace, and placed it in her hand. The absence of this bead from the necklace, I vowed, would serve as my reminder that my heart could never again be complete." He looked again at the necklace in his hand and fingered it once more. Then he slipped it into the pocket of his new robe.

"Go to bed now, Grandfather Liu," Su spoke gently. "It is nearly Christmas morning, a time when miracles happen for children and those who are able to be children again, if only for a day. Perhaps you will awaken with a lighter heart, on the wings of the Spirit of Christmas. You have shared your burden with one who will share it with no one else. I pray for the Spirit of Christmas to fill the empty place in your heart." With that, she left for her own bed next to her husband.

❄ ❄ ❄

Children all around the world were up early Christmas morning, and Li and Sam were no different. Each ran to his or her pile of gifts and removed the wrapping as a hurricane scatters anything not bolted down. Xiang had a gift for Su, and she, one for him. Grandfather smiled at the Christmas commotion, and indeed, his mood seemed lighter.

When all the gifts had seemingly been opened, Li spotted a small box nearly hidden under the back branches of the blue spruce. She dug it out and held it up for all to see.

The box was wrapped in paper decorated with dragons' heads and Chinese characters. It was yellow and blue with a traditional Christmas name tag attached. The tag, read by Li, was addressed to Grandfather Liu. She hurriedly moved to his chair and offered it to him.

The old man was startled and muttered, "It must be a mistake. I have my new robe."

"Open it, Grandfather," Li pleaded. "It has your name on it."

Obediently, he did. And inside was a green bead, embossed with gold, a perfect match for the one that had at one time graced the necklace now in his robe pocket. "But how can this be?" he asked. "I . . ."

Quickly, Su moved to his side. "What a beautiful green bead!" she exclaimed. "It looks to me to be a match for the beads on the necklace I have seen when I straightened your room. Do see if it is."

Grandfather slowly lifted the necklace from the pocket of his robe. "Ah," Su said. "It is perfect for the necklace, and I see the necklace has no other bead of this color."

"But who gave it?" Xiang asked. "Is there no name on the tag?"

Su looked carefully. "Sorry, no name. It must have been delivered by the Spirit of Christmas," she laughed. "Accept it as that, Grandfather Liu."

That afternoon, Grandfather restrung the necklace so that the new bead was at the mid-point of the other beads; and before the evening meal he fastened the necklace around Li's neck. "Your grandmother would want it so," he said. "Let us say no more of it," he smiled. "Now I, too, have the Christmas Spirit." Everyone laughed, except Sam who was asleep in his highchair.

As Xiang and Su were preparing for bed, Xiang asked for an explanation. "Why the bead? And where did you get it? I know it was you. I recognized the paper from the packaging our fortune cookies come in. What's the mystery?"

"You are right," Su confessed. "It was my gift to your father. But please, let him think whatever he likes about where it came from. You saw how it pleased him."

"Yes, but how the perfect match for the necklace? And why did he have the necklace? And why give it to Li?"

Su explained. "Before my father, Henry, came to America, he was a vendor of odds and ends on the streets of Beijing. He brought a box of the jewelry he sold in China to America, thinking he would sell it on the streets here. We have a dozen or more of those necklaces in a box in our attic. One of them now is missing a green bead embossed with gold."

"But . . ." Xiang paused. "What else?"

"The rest is your father's business, and if he chooses to tell us, he will. For now, enough has been said. Go to sleep, and may the Spirit of Christmas give us all pleasant dreams."

And the Spirit of Christmas did just that. It found each room and blessed all in their beds with good dreams, especially Grandfather Liu, who saw a beautiful woman wearing a necklace with a gold-embossed green bead that sparkled like sand on a sunny beach.

He took her outstretched hand and smiled at her. She smiled back with eyes of love and forgiveness. And the Spirit of Christmas smiled also.

# *Christmas Light*

IT'S DECEMBER 7, 1941, A Sunday afternoon. You and Pa are listening to the radio. You aren't paying much attention as you play with your Lincoln Logs on the flowered-linoleum covered floor. You are building a fort, a U.S. Cavalry outpost. A place to which the Lone Ranger and Tonto are racing to report the Apaches are on another warpath. Just like the episode you saw in the serial at the Fox Theater yesterday—just before the main feature with Abbot and Costello, who made you laugh so hard you almost peed your pants.

"Listen," Pa says. "Everybody listen! The president's talkin'!"

"FDR?" Ma asks from the kitchen.

"Who else?" Pa answers.

And the president talks about the Japanese attacking Pearl Harbor that morning.

"What the hell." Pa says in almost a whisper. "Damned if we ain't at war."

Then, one after another, all the boys in the neighborhood go off to war in France or England or Italy or to islands in the South Pacific nobody ever heard of. And Pa gets a deferment because now the factory he works in is making parts for submarines instead of for Ford cars. He wants to go fight "Japs" and "Nazis" too, but he's foreman of an assembly line and is "indispensable" for training and supervising the women stepping in for the men.

And a year later, you are peddling newspapers on Bill Gottshalk's old route. Billy got killed in France, a place he never thought he'd get to see. "At least he got to see Paris," his ma says to a neighbor who stops by when she sees the flag with the gold star in Gottshalk's window.

All along your paper route flags are hanging in windows, most with blue stars. Here and there, flags with gold stars are hanging. The women who sadly but proudly hung the flags with gold stars are called Gold Star Mothers and ride in the newest cars in town for all the parades. You know most of them, and you remember their boys who played football and basketball on the high school teams.

A lot of things have changed because of the war. Rubber has been replaced with canvas for your overshoes. The Big Three are making planes and warships instead of cars. Lucky Strike Green went to war. In the movies cowboys and Indians shooting each other have been replaced by American soldiers shooting Japs and Nazis. And the *Lone Ranger* serial has been replaced by *The Eyes and Ears of the World* with mostly pictures of the war and the war effort, narrated by Lowell Thomas, all for ten cents. Food is scarce and gasoline is scarcer—both are rationed, and a huge black market for ration stamps is flourishing. In one way or another everybody has joined or been forced into the war effort.

You sell defense stamps to the customers on your Eagle Star route. Ten or twenty-five cents apiece, with a free book to paste them in. When your book has eighteen dollars and seventy-five cents worth of stamps, you can trade it in for a war bond for which the government promises to pay you twenty-five dollars in ten years. Every Friday you dismount your bike, knock on doors, and collect twenty cents for the paper. Then you punch the date on a card so you can't try to collect twice, or your customers can't say they paid when they didn't. After that you ask, "Any defense stamps this week, Mrs. Gottshalk?"

All this collecting takes place in the doorway or just inside the house, so you can always hear the radio playing. Radios play all day long, just in case news of the war comes on. Otherwise, it's just music. You hear so much radio music, you know all the words to songs like *G.I. Jive, To Each His Own, Lili Marlene, Ole Buttermilk Sky, Elmer's Tune, I'll Be Seeing You* and *White*

*Cliffs of Dover*. And nobody misses the evening news with Walter Winchell's staccato delivery and a telegraph key clicking in the background. Or Gabriel Heatter with, "Ah, there's bad news tonight," or "good news" if the war is going well.

Your customers leaf through the paper to find Ernie Pyle's column reporting news from the front. And his two cartoon characters, Willie and Joe, crouched in a foxhole, all muddy and wet with rain pouring down on their GI helmets. "You know, Willie," Joe says. "It does sound like rain on a tin roof."

The times are dark and cloudy, but Christmas, like the eastern sky, always brings light. It would be downright unpatriotic not to celebrate Christmas, because celebrating Christmas is one of the things we are fighting to preserve.

The stores are a little short of toys to buy, but Santa's workshop and elves always come through with something. Why, just take a look at yourself:

*A girl (or boy)*
*Searching for that special toy.*
*The tree is trimmed.*
*Its lights are bright.*
*Can't you see that Christmas sight?*
*It's long ago*
*When you were young.*
*Your grown-up song is yet unsung.*
*Hear the bells?*
*It's Christmas day.*
*You've asked for toys, so you can play.*
*Santa's come!*
*Don't you see*
*All the presents 'round your tree?*

Of course you see them. Each giftwrapped in tissue paper—white mostly, but some green and some red. And tied with colored string. A name tag on each so you don't unwrap a doll instead of a Roy Rogers gun and holster set. Or a dump truck instead of a mirror, brush, and comb set. Not even war can stop Christmas from coming or Pa from buying Ma another bottle of Evening in Paris perfume.

You rush to find which presents are yours. Strings pop, tissue paper floats to the floor and settles in multicolored drifts. You open the gift you wanted most. Santa read your letter. What a merry Christmas. And you forget about the war.

Time for breakfast. Always something special for Christmas morning. Waffles maybe, with no limit on the maple syrup. Eggs and ham if you know a farmer nearby. Chances are Mother has a fresh-baked stolen fruitcake or kuchen. And, of course, decorated sugar cookies shaped like stars, bells and wreaths. A lot of sugar and butter ration stamps had to be spent for those.

Off to church now, without Pa 'cause he went to midnight services. Every year you hear the same story. You know it by heart: A baby born in a stable. But not just any baby. This one is God Himself. No heat in the stable, so the animals keep Him warm. Angels in the sky—*Hark the Herald Angels Sing*. A huge star in the sky spotted by three kings who trace it to the stable. *We Three Kings of Orient Are*, a virgin birth. *"Round yon virgin, mother and child."* It's years before you know what "virgin birth" means, but you take comfort in it all. It's Christmas, and Christmas requires faith—faith in the preacher, faith in Santa Claus, faith in the rightness of war. *Oh Come All Ye Faithful*.

*Church gets long*
*Try not to sleep.*
*Eyelids heavy.*
*Sinking deep.*
*Pinch yourself.*
*Give a shake.*
*You felt that pinch.*
*Now stay awake!*

"Let us pray," your pastor says, "for our men and women in uniform, in Germany, France, Italy, Iwo Jima. On land or sea or in the air. Fighting, offering their lives so we may live free. As Jesus died to save us from eternal damnation." You bow your head and ask God to stop the war—*please*. Because it's Christmas, and Jesus is the Prince of Peace. And the war is screwing up everyone's life. Amen.

Christmas afternoon and evening are for playing games,

visiting, shelling and eating nuts, sucking on hard candy, and gobbling down the apples and oranges Santa left in your stocking. The evening radio is all music and static, maybe a little news. Eddie Cantor, Fibber McGee and Molly, Jack Benny, Bob Hope, and Red Skelton, your favorite programs are not on Christmas night. It's a peaceful time. *Oh little town of Bethlehem, how still we see thee lie.* The war doesn't exist. You're getting bored when someone knocks on the front door.

Everyone runs to open it, thinking Grandma and Grandpa are finally here with their gifts. But it's Ellen Kramer with bad news. Rusty Schmidt's plane was shot down in the South Pacific. Rusty was class salutatorian and a hell of a basketball player. "God rest ye merry gentlemen."

And so it goes until the war ends August 15, 1945. Mrs. Myers, who owns the corner grocery store, is crying and telling everybody the war's over when you stop in there to buy some penny candy to eat on your paper route. Another war to end all wars has just ended. No more war next Christmas! *Peace on earth. Good will toward men.*

So World War II is ended, but our story is not. We, you and I, have a beginning and a middle, but no ending. Here we are in the year 1945 with a Christmas story to finish. Any ideas? It has to be uplifting. Nobody wants a Christmas story with a sad ending.

As I think about it, this is going to be a tough story to end.

So maybe we should settle for an optimistic conclusion. One that ties it all together. Let's try one. How about something like this:

So World War II ended. But it was not the war to end all wars. We brought the curtain down, but it was to rise again and again—and again. The actors and sets changed, but the final curtain was never final. There has always been another war waiting in the wings. Yet each final curtain brought hope and faith that it would be the last war story on the stage. And Christmas helps us keep that hope and faith alive.

Christmas is a light that even war has not extinguished. Even in wartime kids write letters to Santa Claus and sit on his knee in department stores. Charity is requested and given on street corners with bells ringing for those needing physical and spiritual salvation. We sing *Silent Night, Holy Night* in many languages in many countries. We exchange gifts, shell nuts, and peel oranges. We celebrate the birth of Jesus, whether we believe Jesus to be the Son of God or a wise teacher with an enduring message of faith and hope.

And in our Christmas celebrations, religious or secular, our spirits join those of the heralding angels for a midnight service, a party, a meal, a day with the family, or a week without school. *Hark! The herald angels sing* . . . and so do we. The Christmas sunbeam somehow breaks through the darkest cloud, and we believe that someday we will sing *We do have peace on earth and goodwill toward men.*

So why don't you and I end this journey to the past with the conclusion that wars may come and wars may go, but Christmas is always coming with an illumination that never fails to penetrate the darkness.

# *The Day Before Christmas Vacation*

TO THE PEOPLE she passed on the street, she was just a plump, African-American woman, stylishly dressed, on her way to some job or another on the fringe of one of the poorer neighborhoods of South Florida.

She became more clearly defined when she turned on to the broad sidewalk filled with colorfully dressed, backpacking high school students headed into Sanberado High School, many from the large and crowded student parking lot on the north side of the the old stucco building in need of fresh paint.

The woman reached the first of the seventeen cement steps leading to a wide and open door and paused to catch her breath, while younger and slimmer bodies whizzed past her like commuters at Penn Station dashing for the 5:37 to Newark. For twenty-two years she had climbed these steps and been jostled all the way to her classroom at the very end of the hallway and adjacent to the student parking lot. The administrator in charge of classroom assignment always gave her that room so that her students' sometimes noisy eruptions would be confined to the same area as the noisy eruptions from jalopies with leaky mufflers. She taught remedial reading at Sanberado High. Her students' frustrations with their failures often burst their emotional bubbles, allowing loud, embarrassed laughter, howls of protest, and the babble of tomfoolery to escape. Among these teenagers were dabblers in alcohol, marijuana, cocaine, prostitution and pimping. The hard core of those who were users, sellers, and buyers had years ago stopped coming to school.

"Willy," as her students called her, reached her classroom only minutes before Leander Love, who was always early and never happy to be there. "Yo, Willy! Whatcha gonna do on your vacation?" It was the last school day before winter break, the politically correct designation of Christmas vacation.

"Yo, yourself, Leander. I'm gonna be home makin' up all kinds of tests and worksheets for you all to fill in when vacation is over." Willy's students had been filling in blanks on reading-development exercises and checking off answers on reading tests ever since they failed the state-mandated test in third grade; yet they still read far below the benchmarks set by the governor, the state legislature, and the South Florida Board of Education. Willy had wonderful job security. As long as there were dysfunctional families and neighborhoods, there would be kids with reading problems, regardless of legislative mandates. And nobody else wanted her job.

Fourteen of the thirty students assigned to Basic Communications—a euphemism for high school remedial reading classes—shuffled, shoved, and slouched into the classroom after Leander. Most hailed their teacher with some kind of seasonal salutation, but none disrespectfully. For many reasons, Willy was their favorite teacher, and to "dis" her would be a lack of class, totally not cool.

"Whatcha gonna read us today?" This question came from LaTania Robinson, one of only three girls in the class. Most girls tested out of remedial reading by ninth grade or got pregnant and quit school.

The question revealed their teacher's atypical approach to reading instruction, which was to read her students stories she thought would reach and teach them in some way. Then she offered them copies of the stories she'd read with the assignment that they read and re-read them. "The more times you read a story, the better," she urged. "Every time you read a story, it gets easier to read."

She answered LaTania's question by announcing she had a Christmas story for them to hear. "Now, you all just sit back and listen." She knew the Curriculum Guide did not sanction the use of *Christmas* literature, but Willy was confident none of her kids would report her. Their familiarity with the principal's office had bred contempt, and they went there only when summoned.

Her students came to order, some more asleep than awake, and she began to read from a magazine whose pages she had read many times before on the day before Christmas vacation. The story is called *Daddy Came Home for Christmas*.

❄ ❄ ❄

*Emmaline Wilson sat in Daddy's lap with her head resting against his chest, as it moved in rhythm to the words of the story he was reading.*

*"There were two hundred rooms in the castle. And on every wall in every room was a large mirror for Princess Emmaline to see how much prettier she was that day than the day before."*

*"Daddy, say it right!"*

*"But that's what it says, sweetheart."*

*"When Mama reads it, she says, Princess Primrose."*

*"Well, baby, I know a Princess Emmaline who is getting prettier every day—prettier than this picture of Princess Primrose."*

*And so it was that each time Daddy read her a story, he found some way to put her in it; and though she protested, she loved his alterations and him for making them. And she loved his oily smell from working at Eddie's Car Care and the feel of his voice beneath his shirt. It was deep and rumbly, like the bottom of a river where the cool water sweeps across sand, splashes over stones, and slips past fishes. That's how Daddy read.*

*Emmaline felt like a character in a story. There was a mama and a daddy, and she was their little girl. Daddy went to work every morning at Eddie's Car Care, and Mama went to work at the Uptown Diner. Emmaline went downstairs to Mrs. Feldman's apartment, where she played with Cora and Manny Feldman, ate lunch, and took a nap. Then Mama came home and Daddy came home, and they were a family again. Everyone was living happily ever after . . . until Daddy lost his job at Eddie's and couldn't find another one. Then everything changed.*

*When Daddy read her a story, he didn't have that oily smell Emmy liked. Instead, his breath smelled funny, and he missed words and said some of them wrong when he didn't mean to. Some nights Daddy didn't come home at all, so Mama read to her, but it wasn't the same. Nothing was the same anymore.*

*One night Emmy woke up and heard Mama and Daddy quarreling real loud. She could smell cigarette smoke coming under the door of her room, and she knew Daddy was being bad because Mama got sick from cigarette smoke and had asked Daddy to please never smoke in the house. Then she heard Daddy using some naughty words that Mama had asked him never to use. Finally, the door slammed, and Emmy knew Daddy was gone. The next morning, Mama said Daddy wouldn't be coming home anymore. He was going to live somewhere else, in a different city, and Emmy should just try to forget all about him.*

*Emmaline's gradual realization that Daddy was not coming home anymore was like nightfall. Little by little, the light faded until there was nothing but darkness filled with sadness and longing for Daddy. But as the sun sets, it also rises; and the prospect of going to school brought sunshine back to Emmy's life. She moved Daddy to the back of her memories and thought of him only when someone read her a story, and then she was attacked by feelings of anger for his having left Mama and her all alone.*

*Emmaline Wilson began school filled with enthusiasm and anticipation. Mama had said, "It won't be long, and I won't have to read to you. You'll be doin' all your own readin'. You got to pay me back by readin' some stories to me." And Emmy thought how wonderful it would be to read Mama a story . . . and even more wonderful to read one to Daddy. She would read "Princess Primrose," and Daddy would ask her to read it again; and she would, just as he had always read it again to her until she knew "Princess Primrose" by heart.*

*But Emmaline did not learn to read easily. And the harder she tried, the more mistakes she made. So she was given more tests and more worksheets with blanks for her to fill in and paragraphs to read instead of stories. She was even enrolled in* a special phonics program where she tried to learn that, when the letter "c" is followed by "e" or "i," it makes the sound of "s." And that when two vowels go walking, the first one does the talking and says its own name, except in words like "bread" and "chief." And hardest of all, when the consonant "r" precedes a vowel, the vowel makes a sound that is neither long nor short.

All of the hard work didn't help Emmy to read sentences when she couldn't decide if "them" was "then" or "was" was "saw." And trying to sound out so many words made her lose track of what the sentence was about. Reading whole stories seemed unattainable. By Christmas of third grade, Emmaline Wilson was certain she would never learn to read.

And that's when Mama gave her some disturbing news. "Your daddy is back, Emmaline. He sat himself down at one of my tables at the Uptown and says, bold as brass, he wants to see you, honey."

Emmy was stunned. She sensed her mother wanted her to say something, but she didn't know what to say. So she asked, not really wanting to know, "Where's he been at, Mama?"

"He says he's been away, and now he's back workin' at Eddie's again. Your daddy always was the best there is at fixin' cars." She paused. "He really wants to see you, Emmy."

"I don't want to see him, Mama. I hate him!"

"No, you don't, sweetheart. He's your daddy, and he's got a right to see his only child."

"I'll run away, Mama."

"No, you won't, Emmaline Wilson, 'cause I got a nice Christmas planned for you and me."

"You got a present for me?"

"Yes, I do. And a canned ham from Mr. Rustin at the Uptown."

"What is my present, Mama?"

"You gotta wait for Santa Claus, but you're gonna look real pretty wearin' it for when your daddy comes." Mama played the Christmas present game, but not with the same suspense most parents applied.

Emmy pouted. "Now you went and told me what my present is." She thought for a moment. "When's Daddy comin'?"

"Six o'clock Christmas Eve."

The Uptown closed after the lunch hour the day before Christmas, and Mama hurried home to get Emmy from Mrs. Feldman's and to get the ham in the oven. Horace loved the smell of ham bakin' in the oven. Let him see what he's been missin' these years he's been gone.

Mrs. Feldman was feeding the new baby when Mama arrived, and Emmy was building a Lincoln Log fort with Cora and Manny. The Lincoln Log set was a Hanukkah present for Manny. Cora had received a more practical gift, new underwear and socks.

Mama opened the conversation. "We gotta scoot, Edna. Company comin' at six."

"Sit down, Pearl. What's the big rush? I have some fresh chocolate chips and a need to talk to someone older than ten."

"Horace comin' by, Edna. He's back in town and wantin' to see Emmy."

"Really, Pearl? When you said 'company,' I was thinkin' 'bout your old Sandy Claws." (Mrs. Feldman was always critical of the Christmas traditions of Christians.) Her face stiffened, and she cautioned, "You be careful, Pearl. Some company can bring along a bagful of trouble."

"Not this company, Edna. I told this Santy Claus he got one hour to say howdy-doo. Then he gotta scoot right back up the chimney he come down in. But ain't he gonna be surprised at how pretty and grown-up our Emmy is?"

"Just remember, Pearl. One hour. I guess even Horace can't cause too much trouble in one hour . . . if he's not drinking."

"He knows better than that, comin' to my house. We gotta go now. Come along, Emmy. Merry Christmas, Edna." She thought a moment, "or Happy . . . what is it?"

"Hanukkah, Pearl. Happy Hanukkah."

At ten minutes to six, Emmaline Wilson was sitting in the big chair she and her daddy sat in when he read to her. She was watching "Wheel of Fortune." The letters coming up on the big board meant little to her, but she was fascinated by how the contestants made words out of them. For some strange reason she derived pleasure from watching others do what she could not.

When the three measured taps on the door to the hallway

finally came, she felt her whole body getting tight. The dress she thought so beautiful minutes earlier now seemed homely and ill-fitting. She wished the door would be stuck shut and the man on the other side unable to get in.

Mama heard the taps too and came running from the kitchen, smoothing her hair as she ran. When she got to the door, she sniffed to be sure the aroma of the ham in the oven had drifted there. Then she slowly placed the palms of both hands flat on the door, as if she were trying to feel the man on the other side before seeing him. Finally, she opened the door with forced slowness.

There was a moment of awkward silence, broken when Mama said sharply, without looking away from the man in the doorway, "Emmaline, turn the TV off. Your daddy is here to see you."

"I come to see you too, Pearl. Now don't let's get nothin' started on Christmas Eve."

"You're right, Horace. I'm glad to see you lookin' so good. Me and Emmy both glad to see you."

Emmaline watched and heard her parents as if they were actors on television. They were framed by the open doorway:

> Daddy: You're lookin' good too, Pearl. I been imaginin' how it would feel. You know, comin' back to the apartment and all.
> Mama: You put on some weight, Horace. Looks good on you.
> Daddy: (smiling for the first time) Eatin' lotta Snickers bars. Gave up the smokes.
> Mama: (feigning a faint) Good Lord! You gotta stop shockin' me like that.
> Daddy: Tryin' to save up a few bucks. Eddie says he might need a partner to open up another shop. Business been good.
> Mama: You and Eddie getting' along now?
> Daddy: Yeah. We work good together. And we go to the meetin's together, too.
> Mama: What meetin's those?
> Daddy: Oh, just somethin' called AA. It ain't

*important*, Pearl.

Mama: *I know what AA is, Horace. And it is important. (short pause) Now, you get on in here and say Merry Christmas to your beautiful daughter. She just insisted on wearin' her new Christmas dress for the daddy who run away from her and her mama.*

Daddy: *Now, Pearl, don't get started. This is Christmas Eve, and a lotta things have changed since then.*

He walked to Emmaline and said, "My Lord. Ain't you the pretty one, though. You remember how I used to read to you in that chair?"

Daddy's voice was still deep and rumbly. The broad smile that began slowly opened his lips and revealed his big white teeth. It melted all of the tightness out of Emmy's back and legs. She nodded her head in answer to his question.

"Well, sweetheart, this here is a Christmas present to you from your daddy. Merry Christmas, Princess Emmaline." He held a package that had been expertly wrapped by some seasonal employee in Customer Service.

Emmaline accepted the gift shyly and, as she had been carefully taught, said, "Thank you" and placed the package in her lap.

"Well, ain't you goin' to open it?" It was Mama speaking, and the implication was clear.

Slowly and carefully Emmy removed the bow, ribbon, and colored paper to find a beautifully bound copy of *Children's Christmas Stories*. Emmy looked at the thick book and felt neither delight nor happiness. Rather, she felt the uncomfortable tightness returning to her body. She could never read this book with its big words and long sentences and who knew what else. Despite her disappointment she forced another "Thank you."

"You're welcome, Princess." Daddy was speaking directly to her. "Your mama probably told you I ain't got much time here tonight. What say I read you one of the stories in that book before I go?" He stopped talking and watched for her approval. Oh, she wanted that so much. Daddy always knew how to ask a question knowing how she would answer. She nodded. "Okay, then. How about you sittin' on my lap like old times?" She nodded again.

With her head resting against his chest, Daddy read "The Animals' Christmas Party."

His voice was still deep and rumbly like the bottom of a river. And he smelled oily from his work at Eddie's Car Care. The time between Daddy's leaving and his return had vanished. Emmy felt his chest as it moved in rhythm to his voice as it swept across sand, splashed over stones, and slipped past fishes.

When he finished the story, he closed the book. "Do you like your Christmas present from your daddy?" he asked. And suddenly Emmy realized she had no present for him. She had a new soup ladle for Mama that Mrs. Feldman had helped her pick out and wrap. It was hidden in her private place under her bed, waiting to be a Christmas morning surprise. But she had nothing for Daddy.

"I wish I had a present for you," she said with such sincerity, it prompted a response. "Tell you what, Emmy. I bet you can read better'n me now. You readin' me a story from this here book would be 'bout the best Christmas present you could give your daddy." Emmaline froze. She couldn't let him hear her say "was" for "saw" and "them" for "there." She couldn't let him hear her try to sound out a word and make a sound that wasn't a word at all. Hear her stop in the middle of a sentence because she was so mixed up, nothing was making sense. Her head buzzed with mortification. She would be humiliated, shamed.

"How about it, Princess? Pick any story you want." He held the book for her to take it. She was terrified. "Any story you want," Daddy repeated.

"Princess Primrose!" She nearly shouted the title. "I want to read Princess Primrose." Her mind was clearing. She knew Princess Primrose by heart. She would fake it. Daddy had said any story she wanted. "I will read you Princess Primrose," she repeated.

She jumped from Daddy's lap and ran to her bedroom, where the book she loved rested under her bed waiting for a reader to open its pages. Emmy pulled it out and clutched it to her chest all the way back to Daddy's chair. Climbing back into his lap, she opened the cover and found the first page she remembered so well. Then she began to "read."

"There were two hundred rooms in the castle. And on every wall in every room was a large mirror . . ." Emmaline's voice was light and floaty, like a cloud moving across blue sky on a summer day. For emphasis and to prove she was really reading, she pointed to each word as she said it. ". . . for Princess Primrose to see how much prettier she was . . ."

And then something wonderful began to happen. As if a magician had waved his wand, what had been hidden took shape and form. Emmaline Wilson was really reading! " . . . that day than the day before. But poor Princess Primrose was not growing prettier each day. Instead . . ."

Emmy began to see a system at work in the shapes of the letters and words, the sounds the letters stood for and the way the sense of the sentence told what a word was. She was really, truly reading, and Daddy was listening, and she could feel his chest moving as if he were reading, not she; and, oh my!, Emmaline felt a sense of power and accomplishment and happiness she had never felt before.

When she finished the last page and closed the cover on Princess Primrose, Daddy said, "Wasn't that just great though! I don't suppose any daddy's goin' to get a Christmas present as fine as that. Thank you, honey." Then he looked at his watch and declared he had better get along so he and Eddie wouldn't be late for their meeting. Emmy felt lonesome for him already, and he hadn't even left.

Mama, who had been spending time in both the living room and the kitchen while Daddy and Emmy were reading to each other, asked, "Where you and Eddie goin' after your meetin'?"

"Why, home and to bed, I 'spose. Christmas Eve's a dangerous night for those of us trying to stay off the drinks."

"I got me an idea," Mama said. "That ham in the oven's too big for me and Emmy. How 'bout you and Eddie comin' here after your meetin' and helpin' us polish it off?"

Daddy thought it was one of the best ideas he'd heard in a long time, and he knew Eddie would like the idea, too. So they did come back, and they brought with them some cold Coca-Colas from the cooler at Eddie's Car Care.

*As a matter of fact, Daddy came back often after that. And with Daddy being off the smokes and the drinks and Mama's tips coming in regularly, they eventually saved enough money to buy a small house in a better neighborhood.*

*Their first Christmas in their new home, Mama invited the Feldmans to eat Christmas dinner with them. Mrs. Feldman brought a chicken, because she knew Mama would be serving ham. And Emmaline read everybody the last part of Charles Dickens' "A Christmas Carol," the part where Tiny Tim says, "God bless us, everyone."*

*Emmaline became one of the best readers in her class, and every Christmas she and Daddy read a story to each other and to Mama. And every Christmas Mama baked a ham; and though no one ever said it, they all knew the very best Christmas they ever had was the one when Daddy came home.*

❄ ❄ ❄

The change-of-class bell had rung shortly before their teacher finished the story, but only Leander was out of his seat.

"That's my last story for you this year. Have a good vacation and don't forget to spend fifteen minutes every day doing some practice reading, so you don't forget everything I been teaching you this year."

Willy always spent part of her instructional budget and a little of her salary making copies of the stories she read to her students, so they could take them home to practice reading. Today, seven kids asked for copies of *Daddy Came Home For Christmas*. She was pleased.

On the way to the office to collect her mail, she passed Manfred Feldman, a social studies teacher. He smiled and said, "If I don't see you later, have a Merry Christmas, Emmaline."

"Thank you, Manny," she replied. "And you all have a Happy Hanukkah."

# Birds Fly Over the Rainbow

THE LIGHT CAME on in her brain, dimly at first, then brighter until it matched the light hitting her eyes from the slim column of sunlight between either sides of the mostly-closed drapes. She reached for a smoke from the pack on her bedside table, changed her mind, and rolled over on her stomach to avoid the sunlight. The sheets were damp and sticky from the Florida humidity, and her head and eyes were sore from the tequila she had drunk earlier that morning. "Another day, another hangover" was one of the standard jokes among the musicians she traveled with.

They were billed as "The Seagulls" and for almost a year had played in the lounges of two-star, then one-star, now no-star hotels along the east coast of south Florida. Louise was The Singing Seagull who also banged a tambourine in rhythm to the music Randy and Russ blasted through speakers wired to their guitars. She had a pleasant voice, but unsuited to the only music her partners knew how to play and incorrectly assumed the patrons in the lounges of cheap Miami hotels wanted to hear. Last night was their last booking. In recompense for her Florida tour Louise had half a pack of cigarettes left, about three hundred dollars and another tequila headache. It was December 17, and she was out of work again.

❄ ❄ ❄

Tracy was one of half-a-dozen kids who waited in front of an apartment building in a housing development on the south side of Chicago. In a few minutes the "integration bus," as it was called by those who understood its true purpose, would carry the six to a "magnet" school in a nearby suburb. The drawing power of Austin Middle School came from its music program, one of the best in the suburbs. Tracy and the other five pilgrims had been identified as students whose musical abilities would be served better at Austin Middle School than at Booker T. Washington Junior High School, two blocks from their apartment house. Their status as members of minority groups would also bring AMC to the correct mixture required for the continuance of state and federal funding.

It was snowing a little, big white flakes, when the bus driver deposited the six and twenty-two others who had been picked up along the way at the school entrance. It was eight-fifteen in the morning, the 17th of December, five days before the AMC Winter Holiday Concert. Tracy would be singing her solo for the concert for the first time in front of the other members of the school chorus today. She was worried and nervous.

Tracy Johnson was the youngest soloist on the program, and the honor of her having a solo part after only four months at Austin did not sit well with some of her fellow performers and their parents. Most of the soloists in the Austin music program took private voice lessons, were in the ninth grade, and walked to school or came in cars driven by their parents. None of them was quite comfortable with the whole idea of bussing in kids from the city, and now to have one of them awarded a solo, well ... "Who is this Tracy Johnson anyway?"

Tracy wasn't really a Johnson. She had lived with Aunt Bess for as long as she could remember, and when Bess married Art Johnson, she became Tracy Johnson. It was the first last name she ever had—and if it was good enough for Aunt Bess, it was good enough for her.

Bess and Tracy went to live with Uncle Art and his two daughters, Marcelle, who worked at K-Mart as a shelf-stocker, and Rose, who worked at Denny's as a kitchen helper. They weren't happy when Tracy arrived to share their small bedroom. But nobody crossed Art, and when he said, "Let 'er in," they sullenly did so. Bess and Art had the larger bedroom, and sometimes when they were all asleep, Tracy would sneak from her cot to the old couch in the living room, where she pretended to be in her very own bedroom away from the lingering cigarette smoke, the snoring, and cheap-wine breath of Marcelle and Rose. She had to be careful not to fall asleep and get caught by Art, who would raise "Holy hell." They were all afraid of Art, even Aunt Bess when he was drunk or lost at cards.

❄ ❄ ❄

Russ showed up at Louise's motel to give her a ride to the Miami airport, where she would catch a one-way flight to Chicago. Randy had hitched a ride to Tampa, where he heard someone was looking to add a guitar to his rock group, and Russ had a girlfriend in Miami he couldn't bear to leave just yet. The Seagulls were history, and Louise had nowhere to go but home.

Home. She had no real home, only a sister in Chicago, a sister she hadn't seen in almost twelve years, a sister who might not want to see her. Chicago. She had seen some bad times in the Windy City. When she left, she promised her sister she would be back in a year, maybe two. She would return when she had made it big, when she had found her pot of gold. "It's our only chance, Bess. Take care of . . . things . . . while I'm gone. I'll make it up to you." Now she was 33,000 feet above Kentucky, pensively rereading an ad in the copy of *Variety* she had purchased in Miami:

*Singers Wanted*
*Lead, supporting, and chorus for revival of*
*"Showboat." Chicago*
*Auditorium Theater. Auditions Dec. 12-19,*
*9:00 a.m. to noon.*

Louise had reason to be pensive. She had made many mistakes as a teenager. "Trouble with a capital 'T'," she would say when talking about her Chicago years. But Bess had always been there to pick up the pieces, even the big ones.

"You gotta be real, Louise." Bess advised her. "Quit chasin' after things you ain't gonna catch."

She wasn't even sure where Bess lived now. Josh would know. Bess cleaned up the bar for him every morning. Maybe she'd stop at Josh's. Then maybe she'd give Bess a call. Maybe crash at Bess' place. "Just until I get a part in *Showboat*. Maybe a lead part. Why not?"

❄ ❄ ❄

Mrs. Howley, Austin Middle School choral director, had spoken privately to her newest and youngest protégé. She spoke with traces of the dialect from the culture they shared, "You got nothin' to be scared of, girl. God gives some of us a special talent, and you are extra special, darlin'. You got a voice like one of God's angels, Tracy. Remember, girl, you got a solo part because you are extra special. Don't you worry about anybody else. When I give you your cue, you just sing for me, girl."

Tracy loved Mrs. Howley. If anything happened to Aunt Bess, she would want Mrs. Howley to be her mother. Sometimes she thought about what it would be like to be Mrs. Howley's very own child.

At Mrs. Howley's signal, Tracy stepped forward. Forty-eight pairs of suspicious eyes focused on her back. It would be the first time her fellow choristers would hear the solo she had been practicing with Mrs. Howley, the first time they would hear this skinny kid sing, this kid, who with two dozen and three other uninvited kids, stepped off the integration bus each morning and invaded their school. Now she had a solo in their Winter Concert. She had better not be too good!

The tension penetrated Tracy's skin. She would have fainted or run from the room had it not been for Mrs. Howley's eyes locked on hers. Mrs. Howley played her introduction, and on cue Tracy took a deep breath and exhaled. "Silver bells, silver bells . . . it's Christmas time in the city."

The words floated into the music room and out into the halls, like soap bubbles breathed from an old-fashioned bubble pipe. They dipped, rose, lingered, and burst as this newcomer to Austin Middle School released them from lungs, throat, and tongue no longer fearful and tight, but moving now effortlessly and harmoniously with the whole spirit of this skinny, black kid from the projects. The forty-eight seventh, eighth and ninth graders listening behind her were transported to an Oz they had never before visited. This kid was good . . . too good. When Mrs. Howley asked Tad Arlington to sing his solo next, he begged off with a sore throat.

Tracy was buoyant the rest of the day. Mrs. Howley's eyes told her how well she had performed. And when Tammy Barstow, another soloist, intercepted her between the school and the bus and begged to let her and her parents pick Tracy up the night of the concert so they could warm up their voices in the car on the way, Tracy accepted and purred inwardly from her classmate's stroking. It didn't occur to her that white folks who drive Lincoln Town Cars would know better that to drive into her neighborhood after dark. Nor did she see Tammy and Tad, hand in hand, stroll off toward the football field for an after-school smoke under the bleachers.

That night at supper time, Aunt Bess was frying up a mixture of potatoes, onions, and hamburger while Tracy struggled with a math problem. Uncle Art wasn't home from work yet. "Sittin' at Josh's, braggin' 'bout Michael Jordan and the Bulls." Bess muttered to the frying pan. Then to Tracy, "Looks like me and you eatin' alone tonight again, honey." Marcelle and Rose never came home for supper. They avoided their father as much as possible and would have moved out had they been able to afford their own apartment.

The phone rang, startling Tracy. Nobody ever called at supper time. "I'll get it," she called to her aunt. She thought, then hoped, it might be Tammy. It would be nice to have a friend call her. Thank heavens Uncle Art wasn't there to answer it, especially after he had stopped at Josh's. "Hello," she half-sang into the phone. There was silence. "Hello. This is Tracy."

"Who did you say?"

"Tracy."

"Tracy?" A long pause.

Tracy thought someone had dialed wrong. "Maybe you have

a wrong number?" Tracy suggested.

"No, no. I think I have the right number. Is Bess there?" It was a woman's voice.

"Aunt Bess. For you." Tracy called and returned to her math, disappointed it wasn't her new friend, but also somewhat relieved.

"Hello." Aunt Bess waited a long time before she spoke again. The pause attracted Tracy's attention. "This is a big surprise, Louise. I got to catch my breath." Aunt Bess sounded strange. "We ain't got much room, Louise. There's Art, his two kids, and me and Tracy. And Art don't care much for company." Another pause. "She's fine. Don't cause no trouble. Smart." Another stretch of silence. Tracy noticed her aunt rubbing her thumb and index finger together, a sure sign she was upset. Then she said in a thin, shaky voice, almost a whisper, "Okay, LuLu, but just for a few days. Art ain't goin' to like it, but okay, if you got no place else to go." Aunt Bess gave the caller their street and apartment number and said, "You ain't far from us." And hung up.

Tracy waited a moment before she asked, "We havin' company, Aunt Bess?" They never had company, and the idea was exciting.

"Just for a few days."

"Who is it, Aunt Bess? Who's comin' to visit us?"

"It's someone I knew before . . . before you were born. Her name's Louise. She's a singer."

"A singer? A real singer with an audience and everything? Does she get paid to sing? Is she rich?" Tracy was overwhelmed by the prospect of having a professional singer actually visit them. "Please, Aunt Bess, tell me all about her."

"No need to. Louise ain't shy. She'll tell you more than you want to know, some of it lies. Now finish your homework while I finish the cookin'."

Tracy returned to her studies, but her head was full of distractions. So much had happened lately. Her emotions swelled and teetered. She was somewhere between now and before on her emotional scale, between anticipation and apprehension.

Her emotional scale tipped to sheer delight from the moment of Louise's entrance, shortly after Tracy and Aunt Bess had eaten. Louise was everything Tracy hoped to become, beautiful, confident, vivacious, successful. She had been with a great musical group that was a big hit up and down the Florida coast.

"A few days ago, I quit the group," Louise chattered. "I was getting too good for them. They were holding back my career." Tracy was spellbound. "Singing for your living is just great," Louise rattled on. "Once Bess wanted me to take a job at Woolworths. Can you believe that? Using my voice to say, 'Thank you. Come again. Have a nice day.'" She and Tracy laughed at the joke.

"A little honest work never hurt nobody's voice," Aunt Bess said from the kitchen sink.

Louise continued, "Then yesterday I read about some openings for singers right here in Chicago. They're casting for *Show Boat*. Can you imagine? Could anyone be more perfect for a part in *Show Boat* than me?"

Tracy could not. No one could be more perfect for any part in any show in any place than Louise. "You'll get a solo part, I'm sure," she assured this captivating creature sitting next to her on their old couch.

Art came home, grunted when Bess told him Louise would be sleeping on the couch for a few nights, ate his supper, and staggered off to bed. Rose and Marcelle came home, shrugged indifferently toward Louise, and went directly to their room. Aunt Bess told Tracy not to stay up too late and joined Art. Tracy and Louise were by themselves.

"Do you like to sing?" Louise asked.

It was a welcome question, and Tracy eagerly related her school singing experiences, emphasizing her *Silver Bells* solo.

"Do you know *Over the Rainbow*?"

"Oh, I do. We sang it in chorus."

"Let's sing it together. It's my favorite. I think people get to know each other by singing together, don't you?"

"Oh, I do."

Louise started, and Tracy quickly joined in, "... *way up high ... why then oh why can't I?*" The song ended, and when Tracy looked at Louise, she saw tears in her eyes.

"Why are you crying?" she asked innocently. Louise stood, took Tracy's two hands, and pulled her gently to a standing position. Then she looked straight into Tracy's eyes for a long moment.

"I'm sad you got to live with Art Johnson," Louise said. "You ain't Art Johnson's daughter, and he ain't your daddy. He ain't even your uncle. Go to bed now, honey. You and me both got a big day tomorrow. We both gotta fly over that rainbow."

❄ ❄ ❄

The next morning, Tracy slipped quietly out of her bedroom past Louise sleeping on the old couch, past the kitchen table where she picked up two cookies she would eat for breakfast on the bus and out the door.

Uncle Art had gone to work already, but everyone else was still asleep. It was December 18, the day before the Winter Concert and the day of the last full rehearsal which Mr. Howley would conduct in the AMC Auditorium. Tracy wished she could spend the day with Louise, but she knew that couldn't be. She couldn't wait to get home, tell Louise about rehearsal, and hear about Louise's audition, which she knew would be triumphant. She wished Louise could live with them always.

Rehearsal went well. Tracy's solo was going to be the hit of the concert. Everybody knew it. Mrs. Howley spoke to her after rehearsal. "A special friend of mine is coming to the concert, Tracy. Sing real sweet, sugar. I told him to listen 'specially for you." In science class Tracy passed Tammy her address and phone number again, just to be sure. Tammy gave her a thumbs-up sign and mouthed the words, "Six-thirty." Tracy wished Louise could meet her friend, Tammy.

The bus ride from school seemed interminable to Tracy. She had made a big decision after rehearsal. She would invite Louise to the Winter Concert. She would ask Tammy tomorrow if a friend could ride along with them. Tammy and Louise would surely hit it off right away, and Tammy's parents would be very impressed. Aunt Bess would never go to any school functions at Austin. She felt out of place in with so many white folks and so few of her "own kind," as she liked to put it. But Louise was different. She might go.

Tracy had also decided to ask Aunt Bess if they could have a Christmas tree this year, just a small one, and maybe some presents. Art had always put his foot down about spending hard-earned money on some "fool holiday," but now, why, maybe he would change his mind. Things were different now with Louise there.

Aunt Bess and Louise were talking seriously when Tracy entered the apartment, and their conversation was not entirely friendly. Tracy had intended to issue her invitation to Louise and ask about Christmas immediately, but she listened instead.

"You gotta grow up, Louise," Aunt Bess was saying. "Ain't no excuse for you sleepin' through a job interview."

"Audition," Louise corrected.

"Don't matter."

"Besides, they were casting for chorus parts today. Tomorrow is for leading roles. I just got all rested up to land a bigger part."

Tracy gathered correctly that Louise had overslept and missed tryouts. Aunt Bess had spoken her mind; now she acknowledged Tracy's entrance. "Lord, you home already? I better start supper." The air seemed cleared, so Tracy spoke. She tried to sound nonchalant.

"Louise, you wanna come to my Winter Concert? I'm getting' a ride with my best friend. You can ride along. I'm singin' a solo, Louise, *Silver Bells*." There! She had done it. Now she waited expectantly for Louise's response. Surprisingly, there was no hesitation.

"Oh, yes!" Louise gushed. "Oh, yes! I love Christmas music. And Bess will come along, won't you Bess? It'll put us all in the Christmas spirit." And she went on about how every family should celebrate this magnificent season. Tracy was once again delighted by Louise's enthusiasm and pleasantly surprised when Aunt Bess, after some good-natured teasing from Louise, agreed to go also.

"If they can stand me, I guess I can stand them," she said, referring to the white suburbanites she mistrusted. "But don't tell Art." Tracy felt her chest swell in admiration for the way Louise had twisted Aunt Bess around her little finger, something Louise had always known exactly how to do.

The two women took turns speaking, making their plans before Art came in for his supper. Tracy was enthralled to be included in real, grown-up female talk.

After she finished at Josh's, Aunt Bess would take the train downtown and meet Louise at Rusty's Roundup, a bar on Wabash, near the theater where Louise would be auditioning. They would eat lunch and then shop for some Christmas presents, just practical things, what people really needed, and maybe buy a few decorations for the apartment. "To hell with Art!" Bess exclaimed, and Louise and Tracy laughed hard at her bravado. Louise, for all her shortcomings, could work wonders on the psyches of those around her. If Louise could fly over the rainbow, so could they.

"Christmas presents, really?" Tracy was incredulous.

"I been saving a few dollars Art don't know about. New curtains can wait. I guess we need some Christmas more." Bess stopped and looked directly at Tracy. "Me and Louise will go to hear you sing tonight, honey. It's Art's night to play cards at Josh's, so he won't be home until closin' time. You fix yourself some supper and go back to your school with your new friend. We'll be there when you sing your solo." Louise moved quickly to the older woman and hugged her tightly. Tracy flushed with emotional warmth.

Later that night, Bess and Louise talked at the kitchen table quietly to avoid waking anyone.

"You oughta tell her, LuLu. She's getting' too old not to know."

"Not yet, Bess, not yet. I gotta be a success when I tell her. I gotta be over that rainbow. Just a little longer, please, Bess. Maybe tomorrow. Maybe I'll get the part of Julie. Imagine, me bein' Julie in *Show Boat*. It's a big part, Bess. It'll pay a lot. I'll tell her then."

After a school day and a bus ride home she thought would never end, Tracy unlocked the apartment door and stepped inside. The place felt cold and lonely. She had wanted to talk to Tammy that day, but Tammy was never in her usual places. Tracy was lightheaded with the excitement of Winter Concert night, but she managed to eat a piece of peanut-butter toast with raisins sprinkled on top and drink a diet cola. She put on her best clothes and at six-fifteen walked to the first-floor building entrance where she waited expectantly for the arrival of Tammy and her parents. She could tell them she would have family at the concert, too.

What seemed like more than fifteen minutes passed. Disregarding the danger, Tracy stepped outside into the darkness to wait. More time passed, and she began to worry. She asked the time of a woman passerby. "Seven o'clock." Suddenly, like being shown the "how" of a magic trick, Tracy understood everything. She was momentarily embarrassed by her gullibility, then shocked by the implication of her predicament: Aunt Bess, Louise, Mrs. Howley, Mrs. Howley's friend, *Silver Bells* . . . she would miss the Winter Concert. She couldn't breathe.

Frantically, Tracy's brain began to search for relief. Could she walk to school? Too far. Take a cab? No money. Ask for help? Who? Uncle Art? Maybe. She ran for Josh's.

"Hey, Art. Kid here askin' for Mr. Johnson. You answer to that name?"

"Get outta here, Tracy."

"But . . . Uncle Art. Please."

"You get the hell outta here!"

"Better go, kid. Art's been here a long time, and he's losin'."

It was all over for Tracy. The concert was already started. She was too scared, too angry, too hurt, too dead to cry. She turned for home.

"Ain't you out kinda late, little Tracy?" A female voice.

"Ain't you scared someone gonna catch and eat you?" Another female voice.

"Who she?" A male voice.

"Our baby sister." Sarcastically.

It was Rose and Marcelle, hanging out on the corner with Skeeter Brown, neighborhood slick.

"I'm tellin' Art you out at night." It was Rose.

"He gonna whup you good." Marcelle

"Why you out here?" Rose again.

Tracy saw no point in keeping her catastrophe secret, so she, with a sprinkling of tears soon becoming a cascade, sobbed out her misfortune. Then Skeeter spoke. "I can get a car. You want a ride? We'll show them smart, white asses."

Without encouragement Skeeter ran off and in minutes returned with a Cadillac DeVille. "Get in," he ordered, and by eight-fifteen Tracy, Skeeter, Rose, and Marcelle were in the wings of the stage of the Austin Middle School Auditorium. "You gonna sing your song, kid," Skeeter promised. With a wave of his hand, he caught Mrs. Howley's eye from her place at the conductor's podium and with his index finger directed her attention to Tracy's presence. Mrs. Howley smiled. Tad Arlington was singing his solo.

When the applause following Tad's *Little Drummer Boy* stopped, Mrs. Howley, without explanation, strode from the stage to the wings. Completely unruffled, she said to Tracy, "You will be last on the program. Sing sweet, girl." Then to Rose, Marcelle, and Skeeter, "Clean her up."

Right after Tammy Barstow's solo and before the final number by the entire chorus, Mrs. Howley turned to the audience. "I am pleased to announce the delayed arrival of one of our soloists. Before the chorus concludes our program, I am delighted to present Tracy Johnson singing *Silver Bells*." There was some polite clapping, and Skeeter Brown shoved Tracy out of the wings. If ever there were a wretched-looking little creature, it was she. Like a scolded puppy, Tracy, head drooping, sidled up to Mrs. Howley's podium. The piano tinkled *Silver Bells*.

Mrs. Howley reached down, lifted Tracy's chin, and quietly commanded, "Sing, girl. Sing for me, sing for your family, sing for my friend, sing for your school, sing for yourself, sweetheart, sing for all of us, rich, poor, white, black. Sing, girl."

And Tracy sang, softly at first, gently, sweetly. And the bubbles began to float, "... *it's Christmas time in the city ... Silver bells ...*" The bubbles sailed and drifted into the audience. They rose, dipped, fell, and burst, filling every space in the room. Every listener's inner voice sang along, anticipating each word and note in the familiar carol.

Tracy sang for Louise and Aunt Bess, somewhere in that darkness. She sang for Mrs. Howley and her special friend, for Rose, Marcelle, Skeeter Brown, and even Uncle Art. She sang for harmony and love and kindness and birds and rainbows. And when she finished, exhausted and fulfilled, the audience rewarded her with a standing ovation.

Mrs. Howley cued the chorus, the final number was sung, and the Austin Middle School Winter Concert was over. It was December 19.

The choristers and the audience merged for handshakes, hugs, laughter, and praise. Tracy found Aunt Bess. "Where's Louise?" she asked.

"Gone again," Aunt Bess answered. "She didn't get a part in *Show Boat*. Heard there were jobs for singers in California and hitched a ride with someone else who didn't get a part." Tracy looked devastated. "She'll be back," Aunt Bess consoled. "She promised. Said to tell you she'd be back."

Tracy and her aunt turned to leave when Mrs. Howley and a short, plump man in a striped suit and red bow tie approached them. "Tracy, this is Mr. Walton, a very good friend of mine. He heard you sing."

Mr. Walton took Tracy's hand in both of his. "Sweetheart," he said, "I'm casting director for *Show Boat*. You heard of that?" Tracy nodded. "I'd like to hire you for a part in the chorus." He cleared his throat and continued. "And I'm also looking for singers for a revival of *Annie*, all black this time. I'd like you to try out for the lead."

On the way to the train Tracy asked Aunt Bess, "Are we going to have presents this year?"

"Seems to me you got all the presents you need tonight."

"I mean real Christmas presents."

"I gave all my Christmas money to LuLu," Aunt Bess confessed. "California's a long way away."

"What's in California?" Tracy asked.

"More rainbows, I guess."

# *I Begin My Career*

IN 1953 WISCONSIN, THE marketplace for English teachers was meager, especially for male English teachers. Teaching literature and grammar was considered women's work. Real men were sought for teaching math, science, industrial arts and for coaching football.

Nonetheless, two school superintendents recruiting at OSTC had my name on their interview lists. One didn't show up because of a late-spring snowstorm that dumped so much snow on Highway 41 north of Oshkosh, even the plows couldn't get through. The other, who drove from a different direction, said he was nervous about his return trip because the storm was predicted to continue southward. So he offered me a contract after a five-minute interview. Being desperate for a job, I signed before reading the contract and before he could change his mind about offering it.

I waved goodbye to my new boss as he sped out of the OSTC parking lot through a swirl of snowflakes collecting on the blacktop. Then I shuffled back inside to read the document I had so hurriedly put my name to.

I was to teach the following:

1. One English class for college preparatory seniors.
2. One speech class for juniors and seniors.
3. Three tenth-grade English classes.

In addition, I was to supervise one study hall daily, direct the senior class play, act as advisor to the Drama Club, coach the forensics team, edit the school newspaper, announce all home football games (with an undependable hand microphone while dragging a fifty-yard cord up and down the field behind me), manage the score clock at home basketball games, and chaperone the junior-senior prom.

For these duties I would be paid thirty-two hundred dollars a year in either nine or twelve monthly payments—my choice. Sure enough, there was my signature at the bottom of the page. I now knew why my employer had beat a hasty retreat. He was even more desperate for a teacher than I was for a job. The blizzard had been a subterfuge.

I reported for work in late August and stood before my first class a week later. I had made it! I was employed and, having signed up for the twelve-month pay plan, making two hundred sixty-six dollars and sixty-six cents a month. Hot dog! I was no longer a desperate man, still poor, but not desperate.

However, I had one more test to pass, possibly more important than my college finals had been. It was the test every first-year teacher in my new school had to pass—an observation by the superintendent of schools, the same man who rushed my signature that snowy day in Oshkosh.

Word had it that he had "canned" one first-year teacher because the kids raised hell in the class he observed. I was nervous because my third-period sophomore English class had more than a few "hell-raisers" in it.

His visitation was always unannounced; but again, word was that the high school secretary was informed ahead of time and, being a good Christian woman, found some way to alert the novice the morning of his or her examination day.

I lit a candle at Sacred Heart Catholic Church to attract God's attention to my prayer: *Please keep him out of my third-period sophomore English class.* That class of mostly farm boys, who were more adept at squeezing milk from cows than identifying adjectives and adverbs, had been difficult to manage from day one. *And please, God, don't let me miss my alert from your trusted servant, Francine.*

My alert came on the Monday morning of the sixth week

of school when I stopped at the office to collect my mail. "How are you today?" Francine sang. I could not have missed it. My eyes must have widened and asked, "What period?" because Francine held up three fingers. My candle hadn't worked, so I gave God one more chance: *If the kids behave, I won't have a beer for two weeks. I promise.*

I worried through my first two classes, and just before the bell for third period rang, my "examiner" slipped into my classroom, giving no more than a quick hand movement to acknowledge my presence. He strode to the back of the room and sat at a desk next to a window in the back row.

My sophomores followed him into the room, playfully jostling each other and talking loudly. When the first one spotted the superintendent in the back row, he began a shushing campaign that spread to the end of the group so that their noisy entrance was replaced by an eerie silence. Our visitor was peering out the window as if a parade were passing in the distance.

When the students were seated, I stepped forward and unnecessarily asked for their attention. No class of twenty-five farm boys with a few girls in the first two rows had ever been more attentive.

"For starters today," I intoned, "we are going to name the part of speech for each word in the five sentences on the board." I gestured behind my back as if I were conducting a symphony orchestra. "Who will volunteer to try the first one?" No hands went up.

*Perhaps*, I thought, *I am being too formal.* So to loosen the atmosphere a little, I backed up to my desk and hoisted myself to a sitting position, hands palms down at my sides and behind my back to support my torso. "Okay. Now who will try the first one?" Still no takers. "Suppose I do the first one," I said in desperation.

That said, I pushed myself upright, swung my legs to the side of my desk, and leaped in the direction of the five sentences on the blackboard. My left foot hit the floor, and my right dove straight into the metal wastebasket beside my desk.

The basket was round with a larger opening at the top than at the bottom. Perhaps it was designed that way to trap the foot of any first-year teacher who might leap from his desk to name the parts of speech in the first sentence on the blackboard while being observed by the superintendent.

With my right foot wedged in that damnable wastebasket, I heard the silence of the room give way to gasps and laughter. One boy rolled out of his desk to the floor. Another banged his hands on his desktop while one of the girls shrieked hysterically, as I tried desperately to extricate my foot from the wastebasket. Then as suddenly as the silence had left, it returned. I looked up as my foot popped free, and I saw the superintendent correctly labeling the part of speech of each word in the first sentence. Then he returned to his seat next to the window and peered out. The remainder of the class went well, and my benefactor smiled as he left just before the dismissal bell. I would keep my promise not to have a beer for two weeks.

During the hubbub something weird had happened. Through the turmoil I somehow made eye contact with one of the girls in the second row. She was not laughing, but rather staring into my eyes, soberly and with an unexpected empathy. I knew her only as Marcella Jacobson, a girl who never volunteered and who lowered her head and shrugged when I called on her. As she left that morning, I asked if she would stop by after school, and she did. I was correcting student essays when she entered the room.

"I want to thank you," I began, "for not laughing at my predicament this morning." She averted her eyes and said nothing. "So how's school going?" I asked, not knowing how else to proceed because of her reticence. She waited, lifted her head as if to answer, then lowered it again. Finally her mouth opened, but no words came. She tried again, and a quick repetition of the consonant *p* emerged. That repetition became a low-pitched growl that continued until she closed her mouth.

I tried to think of something comforting to say. But I could not. So I said the obvious, "You stutter. And you felt sorry for me. You knew how I felt." She nodded. "Thanks," I said. "See you tomorrow." And that was that. I felt hugely inadequate.

All faculty members took their turns supervising after-lunch activities in the gymnasium. Two-thirds of our students were bussed in from area farms and recreated in the gym after they had eaten. The girls in their angora sweaters, long pleated skirts, bobby socks, and saddle shoes danced together at one end of the gym. The boys at the other end shot buckets, pushed and shoved each other, and taunted the girls. Young males tend to deny themselves many joys of life by scorning what only their gender considers unmanly.

Marcella was a "townie," but she ate lunch at school so that she could dance in the gym with Iris Doyle. Together, they outshone all the other dancing pairs. Although the more popular girls pretended not to notice, I sensed some envy. The thought came to me that the rhythm absent in Marcella's speaking had been routed to her body movements on the dance floor. She was good.

Early in November I realized I had not yet called a meeting of the Drama Club, so I had Francine issue a call-to-meeting at morning announcements. Twelve girls and two boys showed up after school. Surprisingly, Marcella was one of the fourteen, her dancing partner, Iris, another.

I knew that traditionally the Drama Club presented a play to the entire student body the last two periods of the last day before Christmas vacation. I asked the fourteen before me about previous years, explaining that this was all new to me. I began to call on one member at a time to get to know them better as much as to get information. One by one, they told me what had been done and how each had participated.

When I reached Marcella, I was apprehensive about her ability to respond to my question. But I asked, "And, Marcella, what about you?" I felt the room tense and watched as most students dropped their heads or fidgeted with a pencil. We waited, and I considered repeating my question or straight out telling Marcella she need not answer, but she beat me to it.

"*Mumumumu . . . mumumu . . . mumumu . . .*" and then an explosive, "Makeup!" She wasn't finished. "And *cucucucu . . . cucucucu . . .* costumes!" Marcella was exhausted, and so were we. But she had come through.

The kids also told me the Christmas play had not always been well-received. "Everybody wants to get out of here," one of the boys confided. "Sometimes the plays are pretty stupid."

"And too long," another added. Then I learned my predecessor had worked with three-act plays.

"Let me think about it," I said. "Next meeting is a week from now. You do some thinking, too."

I was unproductively thinking about the Drama Club Christmas play the next noon hour when I walked past the gym and looked in. Marcella and Iris were dancing like professionals. *What a pity*, I thought, for Marcella's natural animation to be so severely compromised in her attempts to express her thoughts. Her stutter was also debilitating to her emotional and social growth. And I thought how much more she could add to our Christmas play as an actress than as a makeup and costume worker.

As I pondered Marcella's situation, whoever was operating the phonograph slipped Frankie Laine's *Mule Train* on the turntable, and my thoughts flipped back a year to Oshkosh, a tavern on the north side of the Main Street Bridge over the Fox River and to Cowboy Billy.

He was advertised as a "singing cowboy," but he never sang a note. Instead he pantomimed popular records, lip-syncing and using simple props such as a small whip, a cane, a water pistol (*Pistol Packin' Mama*), dark glasses, and a cardboard cutout of a white cloud shedding tears for Johnny Ray's latest. He worked at the far end of the bar, wearing blue jeans, checkered shirt, red neckerchief, and a cowboy hat. It was a first for Oshkosh—maybe the world. And customers flowed in faster than Chief Oshkosh could flow out of the taps. Cowboy Billy took requests and drank Chief Oshkosh himself until his lips were two or three words behind those of Eddie Fisher, Nat King Cole, Patti Page, Perry Como, and others of the day.

When *Mule Train* concluded, I had a plan. Why not? Perhaps my new school was ready for a new kind of Drama Club Christmas program—a one-act play instead of a three-act. Oral readings of selected excerpts from Charles Dickens' *A Christmas Carol* and a choral reading of *'Twas The Night Before Christmas,* wherein a sophomore stutterer could lip-sync and never be noticed, and best of all, record pantomimes by Marcella Jacobson and Iris Doyle. Why not, indeed?

And so it came to pass. The one-act play did not try the patience of three hundred high school students, almost-released for Christmas vacation, as the three-act play had. The two boys, who in the spring turned out for my forensics team, wore costumes and injected humor into their readings of Scrooge and the ghosts of Christmases past, present, and future.

Marcella stood in the back row for the choral reading, and whether she actually spoke or lip-synced as I suggested she might will always be known only by her.

But neither the play, the readings of Dickens, nor the choral reading was the show-stopper. Marcella Jacobson's pantomime of *All I Want For Christmas Is My Two Front Teeth* was. It brought standing applause. And she followed that by a quick costume change to pajamas for *I Saw Mommy Kissin' Santa Claus*. Then she and Iris and one of the boys as Alvin, Theodore, and Simon cavorted in pantomime to *The Chipmunk's Christmas Song*. That brought two encores.

When the curtains closed, Marcella and Iris danced to *The Chipmunk's Christmas Song* backstage while the other Drama Club members, a few teachers, and the superintendent clapped their hands in time to the music. No sophomore stutterer ever had a merrier Christmas. Nor did any first-year high school English teacher.

❄ ❄ ❄

The format of the Christmas program remained the same for the years I remained at that school, and Marcella repeated her show-stopping performances.

She elected my college-English class her senior year. I didn't notice her stutter had improved, but she was well-liked and had a small circle of close friends. I remember she was very active in scouting.

I do recall she enrolled at a small, liberal arts college after her high school graduation. She was not a strong student in high school, but I encouraged her to give college a try. I believe she finished.

Ironically, the year after Marcella graduated, the school district hired a speech therapist. I don't know what became of Cowboy Billy.

# *The Christmas Truce of 2017*

A FRIEND OF mine, now retired from the UW-Madison history department, once remarked that most of history was unanticipated. And I suppose "The Christmas Truce of 2017" was as well. However, historians will point to signs and signals that the table was being set for a Christmas war years before the actual outbreak of hostilities.

A mood of fear and anxiety had invaded the United States of America. Some prognosticators were even proclaiming the apocalypse was imminent. The fifty states of America were severing their ties of unity.

Deep divisions of aspirations, beliefs, value, trust, and sense of well-being penetrated the psyche of the American populace. Anger and attack were replacing tolerance and compromise. Political parties chose to fight rather than spar. Management and labor left the bargaining table. People disagreeably disagreed on everything from the sale and ownership of guns to whether same-sex marriages would be encouraged or outlawed. The news of the day was a litany of one side against the other. One television network advocated for one side. Another network for the other. It was an adversarial mentality. Points of view and prejudices were so ingrained, neither side could see through the lenses of the other.

Protests in the streets were becoming commonplace. And the growing unpredictability and severity of the weather fertilized the neuroses, psychoses, and phobias of the population. Even those who debunked global warming admitted the weather was raising hell with the crops and wondered where the next damn flood, tornado, or hurricane would deposit its destructive load. The United States was a tinder box waiting for a spark.

That spark appeared when a popular televangelist preached the unholiness of Christmas secularity. "God," he preached, "is offended, as only God can be offended, by the likes of *Frosty the Snowman, Rudolf the Red-Nosed Reindeer, Chestnuts Roasting on an Open Fire,* Santa Claus, and all the other secularities that detract from the true meaning of Christmas." God was angry, he declared, and the changing and violent weather was "a precursor of greater calamities from God's storehouse of retribution." Santa Claus, even if he were called Saint Nick, had to go!

The message so appealed to two U.S. senators that they drafted a bill to outlaw all expression of Christmas that deviated in "any way, shape, form, or manner" from Christian doctrine as presented in the Holy Bible. The bill also required a manger scene inside and outside every building erected and supported by taxpayers from All Saints Day until Epiphany. Money flowed into their campaign chests. Finally, someone was doing something about the secularization of Christmas.

In response, two senators in opposition introduced a bill that outlawed all manger scenes inside or outside any building in the country, including tax-exempt churches, at any time of the year. Their bill also required the federal government to reimburse the cost of postage to anyone on Medicare who sent a letter to Santa Claus. They were likewise deluged with support, and all television networks immediately assembled political junkies to serve on panels for talk show hosts to interview. Radio political pundits sent their staffs scurrying to thesauruses to stockpile pejorative adjectives and participles. This looked to be a fight to the finish.

Of course, groups of protestors and advocates for both camps chartered buses to Washington for marches on the White

House. This strained the law enforcement resources since many, perhaps most, of the marchers were carrying weapons, openly or concealed, as was their right under the second amendment. Turmoil and dissension over the celebration of Christmas spawned boycotts of both *I'm Dreaming of a White Christmas* and *Little Town of Bethlehem*. Department stores decided to eliminate music for the holiday/holy day. The country was at a paralyzing impasse.

Then the "unanticipated" my former colleague in the history department spoke about happened. It happened in the form of a letter to the editor that appeared in a local newspaper. Here it is:

❄ ❄ ❄

*I am really upset about all this hullabaloo about Merry Christmas and Happy Holiday. The Christmas holiday is about the birth of a baby, divine, but also human.*

*I have mothered four children, grandmothered nine, and great-grandmothered four—so far. Babies love everything that doesn't hurt them and everybody who is loving to them. And so it must have been with the Baby Jesus. He would have laughed at "Rudolf the Red-Nosed Reindeer" and performed pat-a-cake to "Hark the Herald Angels Sing." With help from Mary and Joseph, he would have said his prayers and also written a letter to Santa Claus.*

*Jesus would not like his people fighting over what he does and does not like. It's bad enough we fight about what is right for us. Let's not fight about what's best for God.*

*My conclusion, after many years of observing God's creation, is that God loves harmony. We are meant to be harmonious creatures, in tune with nature and with each other. So as long as "Merry Christmas" and "Happy Holidays" are harmonious with the spirit of God's love for us and our love for Him and for each other, let's not go to war over the birth of Jesus.*

❄ ❄ ❄

Some of the larger newspapers reprinted the letter, and eventually it made its way to television and radio talk shows, where panels of pundits of every sort argued its merits.

The protest groups soon disbanded, and the two Senate bills were sent to committees to evaporate. Mangers and depictions of Santa Claus stood side by side. Department stores played *Silent Night* and *Santa Claus Is Comin' to Town*. One church went so far as to include elves and reindeer from the North Pole in their traditional manger scene. It was a miracle, "The Christmas Truce of 2017." And that's what it will be called in the new history books.

*Study, for ignorance is darkness,*
*And study lights our minds.*
*Speak, for voices shape our days,*
*And words keep us connected.*
*Forgive, for malice is bondage,*
*And forgiveness set us free.*

# Acknowledgments

To Carole Sanders, who encouraged me to write this book, advised me on its organization, and typed the manuscript.

To Marie Bone, who was the typist for the stories in this book before they were collected and organized for publication. Her editorial suggestions were always helpful.

To my family, friends, and neighbors who read my Christmas stories through the years and encouraged me to continue writing them and to publish them someday.

To the Perico Bay Club Book Discussion Group, who included my stories in their discussions and did oral reading of excerpts at a Christmas party I will never forget.

To Ma and Pa, who never forgot to celebrate Christmas in good times and in bad. There were some things I didn't have, but I always had a good Christmas.

And finally to Sister Germaine, a real character in the Introduction to this book. She was responsible for my discovery in the third grade that writers and their readers can celebrate Christmas together, no matter how far apart they are.

# *About the Author*

Dr. Richard J. Smith is Professor Emeritus, University of Wisconsin, Madison and recipient of the school's Distinguished Teaching Award. He is author or co-author of five college textbooks and various curriculum materials that include his original poetry, essays, and short stories. In addition, he has published numerous articles in professional journals for teachers and school administrators. He resides with his wife of sixth-four years at Westminster Retirement Community, Bradenton, Florida, where he is a featured writer for the community newspaper. His latest book, *Life After Eighty*, published in 2016, is his personal perspective of living well and staying happy while growing older.